WRATH OF THE
DRAGON CZAR

AEGIS OF MERLIN BOOK 5

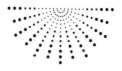

JAMES E WISHER

SANDHILL PUBLISHING

Edited by: Jannie Linn Dullard
Cover Art by: Paganus
0813201701
ISBN:978-1-945763-17-5

BODYGUARD

Conryu roared down the highway on his bike, wind in his face and bugs in his teeth, and the roar of the motor in his ears. The summer sun blazed overhead and the floating island had drifted far off the coast, nothing but an unpleasant memory.

He couldn't think of a better way to spend his second to last day of vacation. Jonny had fully recovered from his encounter with Lady Raven and was back at the military academy. Shame they couldn't have hung out a little longer, but it wasn't to be.

Maria and Kelsie were shopping for new shoes at the East Shore Mall. Conryu would have just as soon gone another round with one of the undead biker things. A shudder ran through him. A month had passed since the near destruction of the city at the hands of the Le Fay Society. The damage had been remarkably limited and the deaths under a hundred.

Most people considered it a miracle and a fair number of those people gave the bulk of the credit to Conryu. Better for him if they just forgot he had any part in the event, but articles kept popping up in magazines and newspapers. Since he refused to do any interviews after the debacle with Kat Gable, some of the reports simply made up details to fit their story. His mother had started a scrapbook and it was already half full.

When he spotted his exit Conryu signaled and slewed across to the off ramp. At the top he eased to a stop and checked the traffic, but found little. He'd waited until well after rush hour to take his ride. Conryu pulled onto the city street and motored downtown. He had a hankering for Giovanni's pizza and only today and tomorrow to indulge it.

Five minutes later he parked outside the pizzeria, lowered his kickstand, and climbed off. He gave his bike an affectionate pat. "Keep an eye on the bike, Prime. I shouldn't be long."

Bad-natured grumbling in Infernal came from his right-side saddlebag. Prime hated being left behind, but he'd been banned from the restaurant for creeping out the customers. Conryu preferred to take him along everywhere, but he wanted pizza and some things were worth the sacrifice.

Ignoring Prime's stream of muffled complaints, Conryu walked over to the door. The smell of pepperoni, cheese, and basil washed over him and set his mouth to watering. The other customers all looked up from their pies when he entered, but soon returned to their food. At Giovanni's he'd never be the center of attention and that's one reason he loved it so much.

"Conryu!" Carmine Giovanni stood behind the counter and waved at him, sending flour billowing into the air. The legendary owner of the restaurant had to be approaching eighty by now, but he showed no sign of slowing down.

"Hey, Mr. Giovanni. Can I get two slices with pepperoni and meatballs and an orange soda?"

"Coming right up. Where are the ladies?"

"Shoe shopping. I begged off."

"Ha-ha! You think such beauties will be okay on their own?" Carmine ducked back into the kitchen and slid Conryu's slices into the oven to heat up. "I wouldn't dare let them out of my sight."

Conryu pitied anyone that tried something with Maria or Kelsie, especially if he found out about it. "I think they'll be okay. Speaking of beauties, how's Mrs. Giovanni?"

Carmine set his slices in front of him and cracked his soda. "The knee still bothers her, but otherwise she's fine."

Another customer entered, distracting Carmine and letting Conryu enjoy his first bite in peace. He liked the old man, but ever since Conryu became somewhat famous Carmine felt it necessary to pay extra attention to him. It was getting tiresome.

"Excuse me."

He turned on his stool and found two middle-aged women in beige dresses standing behind him. One of them clutched a book to her chest.

Conryu maintained a scrupulously neutral expression. "Can I help you ladies?"

The one with the book thrust it at him. "Can we have your autograph?"

Conryu gave the book's cover a look of distaste. *Merlin Reborn* by Professor Angus McDoogle. His unofficial biography. If he ever got a hold of Angus, he would beat him over the head with that stupid book.

"Sure, do you have a pen?"

Of course they did. He scrawled his name across the first page and handed it back.

"Thank you so much." They retreated to their table giggling like schoolgirls.

Conryu returned to his lunch and was halfway through the second slice when his cell rang. He dug his phone out and frowned when he saw the Department's number on the screen. What did they want now?

"Hello?"

"Conryu," Mr. Kane said. "I was hoping we could have a chat. Are you free this afternoon?"

"Yeah, until four, then I've got to help Dad with the late class."

"That's fine. Where are you now?"

"Having lunch."

"Giovanni's, huh? That's only half a mile from the Department. Why don't you swing by when you finish? I'll tell my secretary to expect you."

Conryu frowned, but couldn't think of a good reason to refuse. "All right. What's going on?"

"I'd prefer to discuss it in person. See you in a bit." Mr. Kane disconnected and Conryu pocketed his phone.

Wanting to discuss it in person generally meant secret and dangerous. At least they'd let him have a month of peace before finding him another job. Conryu took a bite, but the joy was gone. He devoured the rest of his food, wiped his hands and face, and stood up.

"What do I owe you, Mr. Giovanni?"

Carmine waved his hand. "Your money's no good here. I told you that a dozen times."

"Okay, thanks. See you tomorrow."

Conryu took his leave and turned toward the city center where his gut told him an unpleasant job waited.

* * *

Conryu pulled into the half-full Department parking lot and eyed the building. Sixteen stories of stone, steel, and glass with an iron pentagram hanging from the front. If not for that little decoration it wouldn't have drawn a second look. Pickups loaded with tools crowded around the main entrance. According to Mr. Kane it would take another month to finish the repairs from their demon battle. They'd gotten the elevators working anyway.

He flipped open the saddlebag holding Prime and the scholomantic flew out. The demon book had shaped a particularly scowling face this afternoon.

"I feared I might suffocate in there," Prime said.

"Do you even breathe? I can't imagine where your lungs are."

"I admit I don't technically breathe, but that doesn't make it any more pleasant in your smelly saddlebag. And before you make another smart remark, yes, I can smell."

"Sorry, but you make people nervous. Don't worry, once we get back to school I won't have to hide you since I'm a sophomore this year and can have a familiar."

"Please don't compare me to some minor elemental spirit." Prime ruffled his pages. "My glory can't be so degraded."

"It's a wonder you can even fit in my bag with an ego that size. Come on. Let's go see what Mr. Kane wants."

Prime flew along beside him as they walked toward the entrance. "Perhaps they found another container and need you to open it for them."

"I hope so. A simple job like that and I'll be out of here in ten minutes."

"Will you join your females in their search for foot coverings?"

Conryu winced at Prime's description. The scholomantic still hadn't fully grasped his relationship with Kelsie and Maria. Sometimes Conryu didn't fully grasp it himself, but at least they weren't glaring at each other all the time. He'd take that as a victory and hope it lasted.

Scaffolding had been erected in the lobby and men in hard-hats were busy repairing the hole in the floor. The help desk sat on the far right-hand side of the lobby out of the workers' way. Conryu waved to the secretaries as he strode past. Everyone knew him now, so he didn't have to stop and check in.

He wove his way past the scaffold and continued toward the elevators at the rear of the lobby. Three strides from the control panel the chime sounded and the central door opened. Out stepped Lin Chang and Terra Pane, hand in hand and grinning like two teenagers on their first date. They made an interesting pair, him in his rumpled suit and her in the gray robe of a Department wizard. They seemed happy.

"Hey, Sarge."

Lin blinked as if just noticing him. "Conryu. What brings you by?"

Conryu shrugged. "Beats me. Mr. Kane said he wanted to talk about something. I thought maybe you could give me a hint."

"Sorry, no clue." Lin shrugged. "There are no emergencies in the city I'm aware of. Terra, you heard anything?"

Terra offered an enigmatic smile. "We're going to be late for lunch. I'm sure the chief's anxious to see you, Conryu."

Terra led Lin out of the building, leaving Conryu to stare after them.

"That woman knows more than she's letting on," Prime said.

"Master of the obvious as always, Prime." Conryu stepped into the elevator and hit the button for the top floor. At least Lin's reassurances about no emergencies took a little of the weight off his shoulders.

The bell rang and the doors slid open. Mr. Kane's secretary looked up from her sandwich. She was in her early forties and had just a hint of gray running through her hair. She darted a glance at Prime, but offered no other reaction to the scholomantic. He felt Prime's disappointment through their link.

"Go on in, Conryu, he's expecting you."

"Thanks."

He walked past her desk and through the door beyond. Mr. Kane's big office was fully repaired after the demon attack. A mountain of papers had built up on his desk. They were so high Conryu could barely see the top of Mr. Kane's bald head.

"Hey. So what did you want to talk about?"

Mr. Kane stood up and came around the desk. "That was fast. Come have a seat. Don't mind the papers. I'm still trying to get caught up."

Conryu sat in one of the guest chairs and Mr. Kane sat in the other. "So let's hear it."

Mr. Kane winced. "It's not that bad, I promise."

"Uh-huh."

"What do you know about the Empire of the Dragon Czar?"

Conryu stared for a moment and gathered himself. Whatever he'd imagined the topic of conversation was going to be, that certainly wasn't it.

"Not much beyond what we learned in school. It's a closed-off country supposedly ruled by a half-dragon immortal. That's all that comes to mind. What's it got to do with me?"

"Bear with me. The czar is served by a force of fanatically loyal wizards called the White Witches. He does something to alter them and no wizard has ever left the Empire. Until now. The rebellion smuggled a young woman named Anya Kazakov out of the country to the Kingdom of the Isles. The journey was a dangerous one and neither of her companions, one of whom was her mother, made it out alive."

"Sounds tough."

"Yes. Well, while she was waiting at the Ministry of Magic's headquarters in London the czar's agents attempted to kill her, again. Several magical creatures smashed their way into the building and killed a number of Ministry employees. Anya survived, but the incident convinced her she wouldn't be safe in the Kingdom. In exchange for some information we wanted very badly they agreed to her demand that she be sent here."

The first glimmer of what Mr. Kane wanted came clear. "You think she's still in danger?"

"She thinks she is and her second demand was that you serve as her bodyguard. She said if the most powerful wizard in the world can't keep her safe, no one can."

"Is she right?"

"I don't know, but her conviction is sincere. The girl's terrified."

Conryu rubbed the bridge of his nose. "Assuming I say yes, what happens?"

Mr. Kane's bright smile annoyed Conryu no end. "Anya will attend the academy as a freshman this year. You'll always be close by in case something happens. Keep an eye on her, reassure her nothing will go wrong. Maybe she'll believe it after a while."

"How am I supposed to protect her and attend my own classes? Is she even dark aligned? If not we won't even be on the same floor of the dorm."

"You don't have to be at her side every minute and the dorm arrangements are a tradition, nothing more. We can easily work around it. So are you willing?"

"She's in real trouble?"

Mr. Kane nodded.

"All right. Where's she staying until we leave for school? Kelsie's camped out on my couch so she can't stay at my place."

"As to that, I hoped to ask Ms. Kincade to stay with us for the next two nights thus freeing up your couch."

"Have you mentioned any of this to Mom, or Maria? Having a strange girl staying with us isn't going to please Maria I can assure you. She's just barely started to warm to Kelsie."

"I'll explain everything, don't worry." Mr. Kane got up and went over to his phone. "Send Ms. Kazakov up, please."

"She's already here?" Conryu could hardly believe it. "You assumed I'd say yes."

"She only arrived a few hours ago. We kept her in a safe room just off the portal chamber." Mr. Kane shrugged. "I couldn't imagine you refusing to help a girl in trouble so I asked the Ministry to send her over. I still haven't learned what Malice got out of them, but you can be sure it was plenty."

Conryu grimaced at the mention of the evil old woman. Other than Kelsie, he wasn't on good terms with the Kincade family. "Is she going on Saturday with us or Sunday with the other freshmen?"

"Saturday with you. It'll give everyone a little extra time to settle in. I am sorry you keep getting dragged into problems not of your making, but given who and what you are you might as well get used to it."

"I—"

Conryu fell silent when a stunning young woman walked into the room. He'd seen his share of babes, but this girl could give Heather James a run for her money. Long blond hair spilled over the shoulders of her white blouse as bright blue eyes darted around the room looking for danger. Pale skin made the circles under her eyes look even darker. And good lord what a figure. He gave a full-body shiver. He was so dead when Maria saw her.

Anya's gaze landed on him and her worried expression vanished. She hurried over, arms open. Conryu tried to think of a polite way to avoid hugging her, but before anything came to him her arms were around him and her chest was pressed tight to his. And what a chest. He gave her a couple awkward pats on the back and hoped she'd let go before he had any excessive reaction.

Finally she released him and stepped back. "Thank you so much for doing this. I've been scared for so long…"

Tears gathered in her eyes and Conryu shot a pleading look at Mr. Kane. He couldn't deal with crying girls.

"Anya, I see you recognize Conryu. Not to be too crude about it, but there's the matter of the password."

"Yes, the password and my blood, that's all anyone seems to care about." She rattled off a string of numbers and letters, all signs of relief now replaced by anger the moment Mr. Kane asked about the password. "They can choke on that cursed drive for all I care."

Mr. Kane jotted it down and nodded. "Thank you and please don't think this is all we care about. No one wishes any harm to come to you, I promise."

Conryu looked from the fuming girl to the awkward Mr. Kane and sighed. Prime chose that moment to fly closer and stare at Anya. She yelped and scrambled away.

"I sense nothing remarkable about this female," Prime said. "Why all the fuss?"

"What is that thing?" Anya asked in a high, anxious voice.

"Prime, mind your manners. Anya, this is Prime, my scholomantic. He's a demon so you'll have to make allowances for his personality. He doesn't have much of a filter, so whatever he thinks tends to come out. Should we grab your stuff and get out of here?"

Anya held her arms out and spun a little circle. "What you see is all I own in the whole world and this was given to me by the Ministry."

"Won't take you long to pack then."

She smiled again and Conryu was nearly struck dumb. Women shouldn't be allowed to be that hot, it wasn't fair.

"About that." Mr. Kane held out a credit card. "It's pre-loaded with five hundred dollars. You should be able to get whatever you need."

When Anya made no move to take the card, Conryu did. "Maria's out shopping today. Could you call her and let her know what's happening? She can better help Anya pick out what she needs than I can."

"Good idea," Mr. Kane said. "Why don't you two get going and I'll tell her to expect you."

Conryu nodded. "Be sure and tell her this wasn't my idea."

"Never fear, I'll take all the blame."

He left Mr. Kane's office with Anya in tow. Hopefully Maria didn't strangle him on sight.

* * *

M aria Kane stood in front of the shoe store mirror and admired the shiny black dress shoes she'd slipped into. They looked nice and didn't pinch her toes too much. Should she fork over a hundred dollars of her summer money for something she'd probably only wear a handful of times a year? She grinned. Of course she should.

"They look really nice." Kelsie sat on a bench a little ways away and watched her preen. Maria felt bad for her. After Kelsie walked out on her mother with Conryu, she'd been cut off from the Kincade fortune. To go from the richest girl in the world to just a regular person had to suck, but as far as Maria could tell Kelsie seemed happy to escape her family, even if it meant being broke. The fact that she was sleeping on Conryu's couch probably helped.

Maria sighed and kicked the shoes off while ignoring a salesman loudly trying to convince a gray-haired woman to buy an expensive pair of sneakers. She'd accepted that nothing would happen between Conryu and Kelsie. Once she made peace with that, she found she liked the girl more every day.

She and Kelsie had been wandering around the mall since early that morning. A stack of bags sat on the floor beside the bench. Maria had treated her to a couple new outfits, ignoring Kelsie's insistence that what she had would be fine.

"So do we have plans for our last day of freedom?" Kelsie asked.

"I don't. Did Conryu mention anything?"

"Not to me, though I suspect pizza will be on the menu."

They shared a laugh. It was nice to have a girl to hang out with. Rin and her family had moved out of the city two days after the attack. They decided living in the country would be safer. Maria didn't blame them, but she missed her friend.

Maria's phone rang and she recognized the number at once. "Hi, Dad, what's up? Yeah, we're still at the mall. Why's he coming? Bodyguard? To who?"

"What's going on?" Kelsie asked.

Maria shook her head, trying to focus on what her father was saying. They had Conryu playing bodyguard for some girl from…

"Where did you say she was from?" Maria asked. "The Empire of the Dragon Czar. Seriously?"

She listened to her father for a minute more.

"Yeah, no problem. We'll meet him out front." Maria put her phone away and decided against the new shoes. "They've got Conryu on bodyguard duty. Some girl the Dragon Empire wants dead. Dad doesn't think she's in much danger this far from the Empire, but she insisted on having Conryu protect her."

"And of course he agreed," Kelsie said.

Maria nodded. "Can you imagine him saying no? All they had to do was dangle a damsel in distress in front of him and he agreed to whatever the Department wanted."

They collected their bags, left the shoe store, and set out for the main entrance. A pair of screaming kids ran past them followed by an exhausted-looking woman that had to be their mother. The mall was full of families buying school supplies. And not just young kids. Sentinel City was sending three girls to the academy this year, no boys though. Maria doubted there would ever be another male wizard in her lifetime.

"If it was one of us in danger he wouldn't hesitate to protect us," Kelsie said.

"I know. It's one of the things I love about him, but it makes Conryu easy to manipulate. And it's not just women, he'd go out of his way to help anyone." Maria shrugged. "It's who he is and I wouldn't change him for anything."

"Me either." Kelsie got the faraway look that always made Maria think she was fantasizing about Conryu. That look didn't bother her anywhere near as much as it used to.

They finally got free of the crowds and pushed through the front doors. No sign of Conryu yet so they went to the car and stashed their purchases. Maria had borrowed her mother's new sedan. The city government had agreed to pay for the replacement since it was their SWAT team that shot up her old one.

Maria locked the doors just as a familiar rumble approached. She spotted Conryu a moment later. He didn't have his helmet on, instead a half-visible girl wore it, her blond hair streaming behind her as he pulled into a parking spot.

Conryu waved as they approached. He put the kickstand down and the girl climbed off. Maria's jaw dropped when she got a good look at her. That was who her father wanted Conryu to protect? Why couldn't he have an ugly girl to watch over? Because Maria was cursed. Everywhere he went beautiful women found their way to Conryu.

Just look at Kelsie. She was pretty enough, but this girl was on a whole other level. She could have been a supermodel for heaven's sake.

"Did you know she'd be that cute?" Kelsie asked.

"No, my father failed to mention that part. I'll have to discuss it with him tonight."

Prime flew up out of the saddlebag and into Conryu's grasp. The girl said something and he laughed. They looked entirely too friendly.

"Hey." Conryu gave her a one-armed hug and kissed her cheek. "Your dad called, right?"

"Yes, though he left out some details. Aren't you going to introduce us?"

"Right, sorry. Anya Kazakov, let me introduce my girlfriend Maria and my regular friend Kelsie. God, that sounds horrible, doesn't it?" He grinned at Kelsie, totally unaware of the awkwardness of the situation or at least pretending to be. "Is there some better way to describe our relationship? After all we've been through regular friend seems inadequate."

"Just friend is okay." Kelsie offered a hand to Anya who looked up from her shoes and shook it. "Nice to meet you."

"Likewise," Anya said.

Maria thrust out a hand. "My dad says you've had a rough time. Don't worry, we'll get you set up."

"Thank you. It was very kind of Conryu to agree to protect me. Being with him makes me feel safe for the first time in ages." She grabbed his arm and hung on tight. "I hope we can all be friends."

Conryu gave her a helpless look. It wasn't his fault, she understood that, but god. If Anya planned to hold on to him like that she wouldn't be able to stay silent for long.

* * *

Anya took a moment to enjoy the feel of Conryu's well-muscled arm in her hands. She'd been struck from the moment she first saw him by how handsome he was. The picture she'd seen in the Paris newspaper didn't do him justice. And the city, Sentinel City, seemed more alive than any place she'd ever visited. Seeing it from the back of a screaming motorcycle might have affected her perceptions.

His girlfriend's glare made her realize she might be clinging a little too much. Anya relaxed her grip, and let go. He wasn't going to just disappear after all.

The four of them marched toward the mall doors. Anya had read about malls, but never visited one. Back home what passed for stores generally stocked one or two types of each item and if you wanted something else, you had to sew it yourself. Anya's mother had a knack for sewing and she made Anya many beautiful dresses before they'd been forced to flee.

Conryu opened the door and held it for them, and she followed the other girls through. He fell in behind them as his girlfriend took the lead.

"So what do you like to wear?" Maria asked.

"Anything's fine. What sort of thing do you wear at the academy?"

"They provide you with an outer robe and you can wear whatever you want under it." Maria looked deep in thought. "Something warm for the winter, a pair of boots…"

Maria went on muttering but Anya wasn't listening. She glanced back over her shoulder to find Conryu in conversation with the other girl, Kelsie. She had a big smile and was nodding at whatever he'd said. They seemed to get along well.

"Here we are." Maria stopped in front of a store filled with more types of clothes than Anya had ever seen. She stared at the abundance. A handful of girls picked through the racks, seeming oblivious to the wealth surrounding them. What must it be like to consider such things ordinary? Anya wondered if she'd ever get used to this new country.

Conryu handed the plastic card to Maria. "I'll leave you three to it. If you need me, I'll be keeping watch out here."

Anya's stomach flip-flopped. "You're not coming in?"

"If you're attacked, I'll deal with it, but I'm not looking at clothes. I can watch the whole store from here. You'll be fine."

Anya licked her lips and nodded. She'd dealt with far worse during her journey here. Conryu couldn't be three feet away every second of every day. She needed to get used to fending for herself. Of course, the last time she'd been on her own she'd had to kill a man. It would be nice to avoid having to do that again. Anya could still see him staring with his lifeless, accusing eyes. His death rattle haunted her dreams.

Maria held out a pale-blue blouse for her to consider. "Have you been tested yet?"

Anya laughed. "In the Kingdom all they did was test me. Blood tests, magic tests, you name it and they tested it."

"What were your results?" Maria returned the blouse to its rack.

"Twenty-five hundred and earth aligned. What about you?"

"Nineteen hundred and light aligned."

Over the course of an hour she picked out three outfits and a sturdy pair of shoes. When they left Anya had a pair of heavy bags in her hands and fifty dollars left in her budget.

"What do you want to get with your last few dollars?" Kelsie asked.

Anya had everything she needed, but was there something she wanted?

"Hey, I hate to rush you ladies," Conryu said. "But if I don't get moving, I'll be late to the dojo. Are we ready?"

"I'm set," Anya said.

"I think we'll call it a day as well," Maria said.

"If you'd like to go back with Maria and Kelsie, I'll be home in a couple hours."

"No! I mean, I'll stay with you if you don't mind."

"Sure. I don't suppose you want to learn Kung Fu?"

2

THE DRAGON CZAR

Traveling by wind portal was like riding in the eye of a tornado, or at least what Yarik imagined that would be like. All around him the wind screamed and howled, trying to yank out his hair and tear off his clothes. Beside him the dragon-blood warriors, Hedon and Victor, didn't seem troubled in the slightest by the wind. Their bald heads and silver scales gleamed in the diffused light. Each warrior carried a heavy backpack stuffed to bursting with the supplies they'd need to complete their mission.

Their guide through this magical portal, a White Witch named Nosorova, appeared as a pale blotch in the madness. Yarik had worked with the witch before and found she had all the personality of a dead skunk.

After a while the sensation of movement stopped and they hung in the empty nothingness of the realm of air. If the place had a name Yarik didn't know it nor did he care to. What he wanted, badly, was to escape it.

"This is the location provided to us by Lady Wolf," Nosorova said. "Remember, capture the girl and return here as fast as you can. One of us will be waiting around the clock to collect you. If Lady Wolf has betrayed us and you're captured rest assured you will be avenged."

Knowing he'd be avenged didn't reassure Yarik in the least, but it wasn't like the witch would care. "Send us through."

She nodded and the next thing Yarik knew he was falling, then his feet hit the ground, his knees buckled, and he ended up on his ass. Hedon and Victor landed easily, their enhanced muscles absorbing the impact.

He looked around at the empty field illuminated by dim moonlight. Nothing but corn stubble in every direction. Not a single house, barn, or tractor in sight. If this was a blind spot in their defensive wards, it would naturally be far from any cities.

Silently cursing witches and magic in general, Yarik got to his feet and brushed himself off. From the inside pocket of his navy jacket he took out a fancy, foreign cellphone provided by the External Affairs Committee.

He turned it on and pulled up a map. They were in Sector Eight, five hundred miles from Sector One where Anya was supposed to be attending the magic academy. According to his information, classes began in two days. There was no way he could get there, scout the target area, devise a plan, and escape before her studies began.

The nearest town was a speck called Trent twenty miles to the south. Yarik hated hiking, but saw no alternative.

He turned the phone off and faced the dragon-bloods. "Time to go."

They each offered silent nods and the three of them set off.

An hour later Yarik's legs were shouting at him, his back

ached, and he wanted a drink. At least they'd found a road, a dirt road, but still, it looked smoother than most of the ones back home. The czar, may he rule forever, wasn't overly concerned with highway maintenance.

To the east the sun had just appeared on the horizon, filling the sky with a riot of colors. If he hadn't been so sore and tired Yarik might have enjoyed the sight.

The flash of headlights coming toward them caught Yarik's eye and filled him with hope. "Hide those scales. We don't want to draw attention."

The dragon-bloods narrowed their eyes and their scales sank into their skin and vanished. Now they looked like normal, if huge, men.

The headlights were attached to a beat-up old truck that would have looked right at home rattling down roads in the Empire. Yarik waved his hands to draw the driver's attention. The truck slowed then stopped.

The window rolled down and the driver, a wrinkled man that had to be in his seventies, asked, "You boys need a ride? I'm headed in to Trent. Don't look like you're from around these parts."

"No, sir," Yarik said. "We're just passing through and ran into a bit of car trouble. We'd certainly be grateful for a ride.

The old man's eyes narrowed. "Where's your car? I didn't see it on my way by. Where you headed anyway?"

Victor made his way around the back of the truck toward the driver's side. To his credit the driver realized at once he was in trouble. He stomped on the gas, but Hedon had the back tires a foot off the ground.

Victor wrenched the driver-side door open and yanked the old man out by his wrinkled neck. There was a crunch and he went still. Yarik grimaced at the unnecessary death, but done was done.

"Hide the body and let's get out of here."

"Yes, Agent." Victor dragged the corpse off to the side of the road and Hedon helped him cover it with dirt and rocks.

Yarik climbed into the cab and studied the controls. Everything looked the same as what he was used to. He should have no trouble driving the truck where they needed to go.

* * *

Roman Orlov, Dragon Czar and absolute ruler of the empire that bore his name, stared at the map spread out over the table of his war room and scowled. The two generals that oversaw the eastern portion of his empire shied away from his angry expression and well they might. Roman had killed men with his bare hands for telling him something he didn't want to hear. Adding two more corpses to the heap, even two of his most experienced generals, meant nothing to him. They could be replaced – anyone in his empire could be replaced – only Roman was truly required for the nation to thrive.

He stabbed a claw into the center of the Land of the Night Princes. The vampires' country bordered his and served as a source of endless trouble, the most recent insult being the smuggling of dark magic weapons that the rebels had used to murder Roman's White Witches. It was time to burn the rats out of their holes.

"Why, exactly, do you think my army can't handle a bunch of pasty-faced ghouls?" Roman asked with mock calm.

"Majesty," General Ivan said. "The enemy is immune to mundane weapons and highly resistant to the witches' magic.

Their only real weaknesses are sunlight and silver blades. Our soldiers aren't fast or strong enough to beat them in hand-to-hand combat and they hide during the day. The moment night falls our soldiers are vulnerable. Without some sort of protection the men won't survive a night."

Roman slammed his fist on the table. "You're the generals. Make it work. We must put an end to them before their interference brings real chaos to my empire. If I can't stop these monsters, the world will think I'm weak. You have one day to come up with a solution or I'll find some new generals."

Roman stalked out of the war room and marched down the wide hall toward his private quarters. Worthless excuses for generals. For all his greatness, Roman was always held back by the weakness of his subordinates. Why couldn't the miserable vampires just mind their own business? Certainly, his hunters killed a few strays that came too close to the border, but that was their own fault.

He punched the stone wall with enough force to bury his scale-covered knuckles three inches deep. It was less satisfying than striking flesh, but it helped a little.

Halfway to his chambers he rounded a corner and found Lady Wolf waiting. He hadn't yet decided what game the woman was playing. She claimed her organization wanted better relations with his empire and perhaps they did, but he seriously doubted they wanted nothing else.

Some people looked at Roman, saw his physical strength, and assumed he was stupid. He loved it when people did that, it made crushing them so much more satisfying. In his almost five-hundred-year reign, he'd seen everything men and women were capable of. At this point little surprised him.

"Majesty." She bowed, showing proper respect as a visitor to his court. "I trust your agents arrived in the Alliance safely."

"Yes, Nosorova confirmed that the location you provided was hidden from their wards. You've done us a good service and we shall remember it."

"I'm pleased to hear it. If I can be of any further use, please don't hesitate to let me know."

Roman nodded and brushed past her. He hadn't figured her game out yet, but he would. And in the meantime he'd make use of her in any way possible.

It took Roman's generals only twelve hours to come up with a plan to invade the vampires' territory. He couldn't suppress a toothy smile as he made his way to the war room. It never ceased to amaze him how well the threat of imminent death focused the minds of his subordinates. He slammed the door open and strode through. Nosorova had joined the meeting. At his command she was to stand at the vanguard of the invasion as punishment for earlier failures. Either she redeemed herself or she died for his cause.

A number of pins now decorated the map, most of them in the Black Sea near the port of Constanta. Roman looked to General Ivan. "Explain."

"Majesty, we've consulted with Nosorova and we believe we hit upon a plan that will allow us to create a beachhead in the vampire's land. We propose to erect a fortress protected by magic in a secure location. From there we can send out hunters to eradicate the creatures as they sleep. As we advance, new fortresses will be built thus expanding our reach. The process will take time, years if not decades to be honest, but ultimately we will eliminate the enemy."

Roman had hoped for something flashier. A massive invasion that would sweep the enemy aside in weeks. He'd have demanded it if something like this had happened during the first century of his reign. Now he had learned patience. Slow but steady often won out in the long run.

"I approve. Requisition whatever supplies you need. I expect your mission to be underway by week's end."

The vampires would pay for interfering in his territory. Roman would see them all reduced to scorched bones.

3
THE ACADEMY

The train carrying all the sophomores, juniors, and seniors, along with a single freshman pulled into the academy platform. They'd arrived a little before dark and everyone hurried to reach the dorm before the last of the light faded, not that darkness presented much of an obstacle for this many wizards. Prime flew above it all with an expression of demonic disdain. At least he stayed quiet, which Conryu appreciated.

Unlike the first time he arrived, the crowd piling out of the train knew where they were going. Mrs. Saint wasn't waiting to guide them to their dorm. That might be a problem for him, Conryu thought as he lugged his and Maria's bags up the hill toward the dorm. He knew where he was staying, but had no idea what the plan was for Anya. You'd think if he was supposed to be her bodyguard someone might have filled him in.

Beside him Kelsie and Anya carried their own bags. He would have offered to carry them, but he only had so many hands. At least it wasn't a long walk and he felt pretty sure there wouldn't be anyone waiting to throw tomatoes at him this year, not with the Le Fay Sorority banned from campus.

"Conryu!" He spotted Crystal waving in the middle of the pack. It wasn't difficult as she stood a head taller than most of the girls.

He nodded a greeting. Crystal was a senior this year and he didn't know if she had any club plans. It would be nice to hang out, but with just the two of them, plus most likely Anya, it might be awkward.

"Who's that?" Anya asked. Her nervous gaze darted all around as if she expected someone to leap out at her.

"A friend. Crystal and I were in the golem club together last year. She's an earth wizard like you. I'll introduce you sometime. She could probably give you some pointers later on."

They reached the top of the hill and the academy campus spread out before them. If someone had asked Conryu a year ago if he'd be relieved to return he'd have laughed in their face, but after the chaos of the summer it was nice to be back. If anything happened here, there were lots of powerful wizards to help him deal with it.

Speaking of which… They'd barely started down the hill when the diminutive form of Dean Blane came charging towards them. You'd never guess it to look at her, but the dean was over fifty and one of the most powerful wizards in the world. She most closely resembled a grade school student in her droopy, oversized, pale-blue robe.

The dean reached them and wrapped her arms around his waist. "I missed you, Conryu. I read all about the fun you had this summer. Wish I could have gotten there in time to help."

She looked up at him and smiled. An almost overwhelming

desire to pat her on the head struck Conryu. Just as well he had his hands full.

The dean turned her attention on Anya. "Ms. Kazakov, isn't it? I read all about your adventures as well. My most sincere congratulations on your survival. Rest assured we'll do everything possible to keep you safe."

"Thank you, um..."

"Anya, this is Dean Blane," Maria said.

Conryu grinned at Anya's wide-eyed expression. Dean Blane probably got that a lot. "Can we walk and talk? These bags are getting heavy."

The dean whispered something and the bags flew out of his grasp. His hovered beside him and Maria's flew over to her.

"There." Dean Blane nodded once. "Maria, you'll be staying in the sophomore wing on the top floor. The monitor will get you settled. Conryu, Anya, Kelsie, come with me. I'll show you what we've come up with."

"See you later," Conryu said.

Maria nodded and set off alone for the dorm. He felt a little bad, watching her striding off all by herself. He needn't have worried. Maria had barely taken ten steps when a pair of girls fell in beside her and they set to talking.

Dean Blane led the way inside and down the stairs to the basement. Conryu's room was the first door they came to, but she kept going to the next one. Conryu frowned. Had there been a room there last year? He didn't remember it.

The dean pushed it open and flicked on the light. It was a twin to Conryu's room, same bed, same dresser, same small bathroom.

"When did you build this?" he asked.

"Yesterday. Chief Kane called and told us the situation." The dean grinned. "It's amazing what you can accomplish with magic. We even added a connecting door just in case."

Kelsie muttered something behind him that sounded like, "She'd better not use it."

It seemed no one trusted him. He took another quick glance at Anya. Not that he blamed them.

"This is perfect, thank you." Anya had a charming smile.

"Great," Dean Blane said. "When you're ready, there's food in the cafeteria. Conryu, see me tomorrow morning and we'll discuss your lesson plan for this year. I think you'll be pleased with what Angeline and I came up with."

The dean took her leave as did Kelsie. The sophomore dorm room was right across the hall from the freshmen so it shouldn't take her long to get settled.

"I'm going to unpack and wash up before dinner," Anya said.

"Okay. I'll be right next door if you have any problems."

Conryu stepped out into the hall and closed her door.

"I'm not sure your females like the new addition, Master," Prime said.

Conryu could only shake his head. On the bright side, not liking Anya gave Kelsie and Maria something else to agree on. As he made the short walk to his room, it occurred to Conryu that no one had mentioned exactly how long they expected him to guard Anya. She seemed like a nice girl, but he wasn't looking for a new career.

He stepped inside and closed the door. A hot shower was going to feel so good.

"Show me the Reaper's Mark or die where you stand, pretender."

Conryu stared at the figure in black that seemed to appear out of nowhere. She, and there was no doubt it was a she, wore a skintight black outfit and a head wrap that covered her hair and the lower half of her face. Only her eyes were visible and they were dark and hard and ready to kill.

Remarkable as the eyes were, it was the sword she held at her side in a quick-draw pose he focused on. He knew that stance. Skilled swordsmen used it to draw and kill in a single move. The woman had been well trained somewhere.

"The mark!" she said in a harsh whisper.

Conryu raised his hand and turned it so the top faced the intruder. The scythe mark the Reaper had left on his hand seemed to have a life of its own. Sometimes it was small and black, other times it covered half his forearm and had a silver blade. Conryu had yet to find a rhyme or reason for it.

The intruder gasped and fell to her knees. Her forehead touched the floor. "Forgive me, Chosen, I believed you to be an imposter claiming the master's favor for yourself. If you wish to take my life I accept it as just punishment for my behavior."

Conryu and Prime shared a look. This girl was clearly off her meds. "I don't think that will be necessary. Maybe you could stand up, introduce yourself, and explain why you're hiding in my room."

She leapt to her feet, slid her sword into a pair of loops on the back of her outfit, and bowed. "My name is Kai and I'm a Daughter of the Reaper. My master sent me to serve our lord's chosen, you. When word reached us that our lord had marked a male on the opposite side of the world I believed it a joke played on us by the demons. Why would the Reaper choose you when we have served him loyally for centuries?"

Kai fell to the floor again. "Forgive me. I did not mean to question."

Conryu restrained a groan. Another crazy woman in his life, great. At least this one didn't want to kill him... anymore.

Conryu slumped on the edge of his bed and stared at the top of Kai's head. How was he supposed to handle this? If he reported her to the teachers, they would arrest her at best and given her personality, he suspected it would come to a fight. He hardly needed to cause yet more turmoil. Better to deal with her himself.

"You don't need to kowtow every time you say something you think I might not like. Why don't you sit down and we can talk like normal people?"

"Yes, Chosen." Kai lifted herself with her hands, folded her legs under her, and sat facing him in the lotus position. "What do you wish to talk about?"

"Let's start with who are the Daughters of the Reaper? Sounds like a death cult."

"We're assassins. Since before the coming of the elves we've sold our services to the rich and powerful. Twice we have been called to the service of a bearer of the mark, a Chosen of Death. You are the third to be granted the gift."

Conryu looked at the scythe on the back of his hand and heard the cold voice of the Reaper. It didn't seem like much of a gift to him, but he chose not to say anything for fear of upsetting the volatile young woman facing him.

"What did the other Chosen have you do?"

"Slaughter her enemies, serve as guards and concubines." She shrugged. "Basically whatever she wanted."

"She?"

Kai nodded. "You are the first male to receive the mark. It's one of the reasons I believed it was a joke. When the news reached us we dismissed the possibility of a male wizard existing. I hope you won't take my lack of imagination personally."

Conryu got up and opened his suitcase. "So are you a wizard?"

"Not like you, but all Daughters have a low dark-magic potential. We focus on using that potential to power our abilities."

"I didn't sense your presence," Prime said.

"No. By infusing our bodies with dark energy we can suppress our life force so enemies don't detect us."

Conryu took a black robe out of his top drawer and pulled it over his head. "What else can you do?"

"I can charge my blade with the same energy and use it to cut through magical defenses. Throughout our order's history we have often served as wizard slayers. Our unique abilities make us well suited to the task. My last and strongest skill is the ability to enter the border of Hell. In that timeless place I can keep watch over you and travel quickly anywhere your enemies might hide." Kai bowed her head again. "I hope my meager skills will be of some use to you, Chosen."

Someone knocked on the door. "Conryu? Are you ready? I'm starving."

It was Kelsie. Good, maybe he could buy a couple more minutes.

"I don't think Anya's ready yet. Why don't you go ahead and we'll catch up."

A moment of silence then she said, "Okay. Don't take too long."

He gave her a moment to leave then turned to Kai. "We'll have to continue this conversation later."

She got up and bowed. "As you command, Chosen. I will watch over you from Hell."

"Wait!"

Too slow. She'd already faded away.

A second later she reappeared, sprawled on the floor, her head wrap loose and her dark hair poking out. "What in the Reaper's name was that creature?"

"I tried to warn you. My guardian demon, Cerberus, inhabits the borderland near me. I'll need to introduce you and make sure he understands you're not an enemy. You can hide in the bathroom until I get back, then we'll handle introductions."

He held out a hand and after a moment Kai let him help her up. She bowed. "Forgive my reaction. I've never encountered such a beast before. I fear my sword would have done me little good against it."

Conryu gave her a squeeze on the shoulder. "Don't worry about it. Everyone has that reaction the first time they meet Cerberus. Well, maybe not Mrs. Umbra, but most people."

"I doubt Lucifer himself would concern that terrifying woman," Prime said.

Conryu grinned. The Head of Dark Magic was the only person Prime seemed genuinely frightened of. He thought Mrs. Umbra was a great teacher, but she did have an intimidating way about her sometimes.

Kai slipped into the bathroom and closed the door behind her while Conryu went to the door connecting his room to Anya's. He knocked then asked, "Are you ready?"

A faint rustling then the door opened. She'd changed into one of the outfits Maria picked out for her, a white blouse and jeans. He tried not to focus on how amazing she looked in them.

"I couldn't find a robe," Anya said.

"They'll get you one tomorrow, after the welcoming ceremony. Technically no one is supposed to know a freshman's aligned element until The Choosing. You're a bit of a special case. I hope you don't mind playing along."

"Not at all. Shall we go to dinner?" She reached for his arm, paused, and lowered her hands.

He sighed in relief. She must have noticed the look Maria gave her at the mall. Besides, it was hard to protect someone when one of his arms was unusable.

As they made the short walk to the cafeteria, Anya looked left and right, seeming impressed by everything she saw. "Everything's so bright and shiny. Back home it seemed the whole world was drab."

"You don't miss it at all?"

"I miss my mom, but other than her, I don't miss much about the Empire."

"Mr. Kane said she didn't survive the journey out. I'm sorry. I can't imagine what I'd do if anything happened to my parents." Conryu pushed the cafeteria door open. Almost a thousand girls in a multitude of different robes turned to stare at them. For the first time since he started at the academy Conryu wasn't sure if everyone was staring at him or Anya.

"My mom's only sort of dead."

They headed toward the kitchen to get trays. "What does sort of dead mean? It seems like kind of an all-or-nothing thing."

"Mom got shot in the Land of the Night Princes. Their leader, Lord Talon, offered to transform her into a vampire. I accepted on her behalf."

Conryu got roast beef, mashed potatoes, beans, and a roll. Anya got the same and he searched the tables for Maria. She wasn't in their usual spot.

"Undeath is a fascinating state," Prime said. "There are

many advantages. It's as close to being a demon as a human can get."

Conryu finally spotted Maria and Kelsie. "You say that like being close in nature to a demon is a good thing."

"Of course, Master. Demons are vastly superior to mortals in most ways."

Anya's nervous frown finally vanished. "You two certainly like to argue."

They crossed the room and Conryu sat beside Maria while Anya sat across from him. "Did you get settled in okay?"

Maria nodded. She'd already finished her dinner. "What about you two?"

"Yeah, we're good. They actually built a new room adjoining mine for Anya." Conryu decided not to mention Kai until he better understood his relationship with her.

"How nice for her."

"Please, please, don't start again. You and Kelsie get along now, can't you skip the angry bit and go right to liking Anya?"

Maria's lip quirked as she fought a smile. "We'll see, assuming you behave yourself."

* * *

Dinner didn't last long since everyone was tired. Maria left first, fighting a yawn as he kissed her goodnight. When Conryu returned his tray, he fixed a sandwich from the leftovers and wrapped them up in a napkin. He grabbed a bottle of water as well before he rejoined Anya and Kelsie for the walk back to the dark magic floor.

"What's that for?" Kelsie asked.

"Midnight snack. Want half?"

Kelsie darted a look at Anya then shook her head. "I'll pass.

Do you know what we're supposed to do tomorrow before the freshmen arrive?"

"No clue. I'm supposed to meet Dean Blane in the morning about my study plan for the year, but after that..." He shrugged.

"I suppose someone will tell us when we need to know." Kelsie paused when they reached Conryu's door. "Good night."

"Sleep well."

She continued on down to the sophomore room.

"I'm all in." Anya stretched, prompting Conryu to avert his gaze. "See you in the morning."

Conryu nodded and waited until she closed the door behind her. He sighed. This was going to be a long year. He opened his door and Prime flew in ahead of him.

Kai emerged from the bathroom and bowed. "Welcome back, Chosen."

"Thanks. Are you hungry? I brought a snack." He held out the sandwich and bottle of water.

She seemed uncertain about whether to take it, but finally she accepted. Kai unwrapped her head covering, giving him his first real look at her face. She could have been Maria's cousin. Same soft, pale skin, dark hair and eyes. Only her short haircut and the hard, on-edge expression marked her as nothing like Maria.

"Are you from the Empire of the Rising Sun?" Conryu asked.

Kai nodded and brushed a crumb from her face. "We live on a small island to the west of the main chain. It's only a mile and a half across and an enchanted fog prevents outsiders from finding it. The first Chosen brought us there and created the barrier before the coming of the elves."

"How many of you are there, if you don't mind my asking?"

"Twenty-two full members plus five more trainees. I can return and summon them for you any time you command."

"Thanks, but I don't need an army of ninjas just now."

When Kai had finished her meal Conryu got up off the bed. "Ready to meet Cerberus? Officially, I mean."

She bit her lip, but nodded.

"Reveal the way through infinite darkness. Open the path. Hell Portal!"

The black disk formed. Conryu took a step, but paused when Kai didn't follow. He reached back and took her hand. Together they stepped through.

The endless darkness beyond the portal looked exactly the same as the last time he entered, empty and all encompassing.

"I've never been this deep into Hell before," Kai said in a small voice. "I can't even see our reality."

A growl filled the air and Conryu turned to find Cerberus staring at Kai with glowing red eyes. He gave the demon dog a swat on the flank. "Stop that, Kai's a friend. She's here to protect me, same as you. She'll be hanging around in the borderland so I want you to be nice to her, got it?"

Cerberus stopped growling and barked, his tongues hanging out as he panted.

"That's better. Kai, hold out your hand so he can get a good whiff of your scent, or whatever it is he smells."

She stepped closer and held out a shaking hand. Kai seemed more a scared girl than an assassin in that moment. Cerberus's central head lowered and snuffled at her palm a couple of times before a long black tongue swiped her cheek.

Kai's giggle brought a smile to Conryu's face. It was nice to see a regular girl under the mask. "I told you he was nice. You two should get along fine now. We need to head back before someone notices I left."

An instant later they stood once more in Conryu's room. Kai bowed, the formal servant again. "Sleep soundly, Chosen, knowing I will be watching over you."

She faded away again. Her head wrap sat on his bed. Conryu picked it up and gave it a little wave. "Forget something?"

A pale hand emerged as if from nowhere and grabbed it before vanishing again. He grinned. This was turning into another interesting year.

* * *

Conryu awoke to a familiar breeze swirling around him. He opened his eyes and found a tiny face inches from his. The pixie was sitting on his bare chest wearing a bright smile. She held a three-inch scroll in her hand.

He glanced around her and found Prime sitting quietly on the table. Since there was no way the scholomantic hadn't sensed her arrival he must have decided to call a truce and thank goodness for that. With everything else he had going on, he didn't need those two bickering.

"I thought you might have said hi yesterday. Did Kai scare you?"

The pixie nodded and shivered.

"Don't worry, she's nice. Is that for me?"

She held out the scroll and Conryu unrolled it. Seemed he was supposed to take Anya to the nurse then go to the dean's office. He sighed and the moment he started to sit up the pixie turned back into a breeze. He trudged to the bathroom and enjoyed a scrub from the naiad. When the pixie finished drying him he got dressed and knocked on the connecting door.

Hopefully Anya was up by now. He hadn't heard anything,

but the door seemed pretty thick, which, considering his surprise company, was just as well.

When she didn't respond after a minute he knocked again. "Anya, you awake?"

Still nothing.

"Would you get her?"

The breeze swirled around him then over into Anya's room. A moment later a shriek sounded from the other side of the door. He grinned. What had the little wind spirit done to get such a reaction?

The door ripped open and Anya, dressed only in lacy underwear, slammed into him. They staggered around in an awkward sort of dance before he grabbed her and steadied them both.

"There's a girl, a tiny girl, in my room," she said between gasps, her chest heaving. A shiny golden cross dangling just above her breasts drew his eye. It had to be worth thousands. Where did she come by it?

The pixie materialized on Conryu's shoulder and stuck her tongue out at Anya, distracting him from the stray notion.

He made a herculean effort to focus above Anya's neck. "She's a pixie. No need to be scared. The teachers use them to send messages, wake people up, and guide us to class. This little one brought a message saying I'm supposed to escort you to the nurse's office for tests. Do you know what that's about?"

Her breathing slowed and she turned slightly away from him, her cheeks burning. "All part of the deal the resistance made to get me out of the Empire. I have to serve as a lab rat for the wizards. They want to see how my blood reacts to magic. I don't really understand all the tests, but I suspect I'll be getting them regularly."

"Why don't you go get dressed and we'll get a move on."

She nodded and rushed back into her room.

"I'll meet you outside." Conryu needed another shower, a cold one.

He left his room and found Mrs. Lenore peeking out her door. She spotted him and joined him in the hall. She had on her black robe instead of the pink pajamas. "Did someone scream?"

"The pixie startled Anya, it's fine. Did you hear what they're going to have me do this year?"

"No, what?"

"I don't know. I'm meeting Dean Blane this morning. She had that evil gleam in her eyes when she said they had a new lesson plan for me."

"You need one, last year was a waste given your talents."

"I thought I learned a lot, especially from you." That wasn't strictly true, but Mrs. Lenore's smile made the fib worth it.

Anya emerged wearing a pale-green sundress. The girl could have worn a burlap sack and looked stunning. "I'm all set."

"See you later." Conryu left Mrs. Lenore and led Anya upstairs and down a long hall to the nurse's office.

He knocked and a moment later Nurse Sally opened the door. "This is a surprise. You haven't come here conscious before."

He grinned. "Yeah, I'm just dropping Anya off. You've got some tests planned for her?"

"Not me, my job is to draw blood. Central will handle the actual tests. They want a sample before and after her Awakening."

"Well, I'll leave you to it. I've got to get over to Dean Blane's office."

39

"You're leaving me here alone?" The terror in her voice took him aback for a moment.

"Don't worry, the nurse will take good care of you and I'll pick you up on my way back. You really are safe here."

"What if something happens?" Anya stared at him, her lip trembling ever so slightly. "They said I'd be safe at the Ministry then we were attacked. Please don't leave."

"If you'd both be quiet," Nurse Sally said, "I can do what I need to in ten minutes then you can be on your way."

Conryu nodded. "I'll wait out here, promise."

"Thank you."

A little less than ten minutes later Anya emerged with a cotton ball taped to her arm. They left the dorm and made the short walk to the main building. The sun shone down on them and a light breeze swirled around, carrying the scent of late summer flowers. Hopefully he could get a hike in this afternoon.

Conryu frowned and glanced at his companion. Then again maybe not.

"This is a beautiful spot." Anya relaxed a little as they walked. "There were no places like this back home."

"What was the Empire like?" Conryu pushed the door open and headed toward the stairs leading to the administrative area.

"Gray." Her blue eyes took on a faraway look. "Just about everything was made of concrete. Most days were overcast. I think the witches had something to do with it. It was like they were trying to suck the life out of you. Mom and I lived in a little farmhouse a few miles outside our village. It was quiet. We had a swing hanging from a tree in our backyard. That house was the only thing I miss about the Empire."

"Sounds nice. I'm a city boy, never spent much time in the

country before I came here." They reached the administrative area and one of the secretaries, a stern woman with small, round glasses perched on the tip of her nose, looked up as they approached. Conryu flashed the scroll. "Dean Blane is expecting me."

The secretary grunted. "She told us you were coming. The dean's office is straight down at the end of the hall. Knock before you enter."

The woman returned to whatever she'd been typing and Conryu shook his head. Looked like he still hadn't won the approval of everyone at the academy. Maybe if he helped save another city.

"She wasn't very friendly," Anya said when they moved a little further down the hall.

Conryu shrugged. He'd gotten used to poor treatment over the last year. "It doesn't matter."

Outside Dean Blane's office waited a pair of soft chairs. Conryu knocked then asked, "Will you be okay waiting for me?"

She nodded and settled into one of the chairs.

A moment later the door opened and Dean Blane's face appeared in the gap. "About time. Come in, come in. We've got a lot to discuss."

Conryu had never been to the dean's office before. It looked exactly the way you'd expect: big desk, bookcases, and a window overlooking the campus. She waved him into one of the two guest chairs. As Dean Blane climbed into hers Conryu imagined a pile of books on the seat to boost her up.

"I think we can both agree that focusing on year-appropriate magic in your case is a waste of time, especially considering you've already mastered some of the most powerful dark magic spells."

Prime made a noise like clearing his throat.

"With the help of your excellent scholomantic, of course." Prime radiated pleasure through their link. He had a lot of ego for a talking book.

"So if I'm not going to learn the basics of the other elements, what am I going to do?"

Dean Blane put her hands on the desk and leaned toward him. "You will study with each of the department heads one on one. They'll evaluate your progress and accelerate your studies as they deem appropriate."

"So it'll be like what I did with Mrs. Umbra only with everyone else? That's cool. It'll be nice not to have to go at the pace of others who are so much less powerful than me. Who are my teachers going to be?"

She grinned. "I'll be teaching you wind magic. Hanna will handle water magic. You'll continue with Angeline for dark magic. St. Seraphim will cover light magic. Callie will teach fire magic. Last but not least will be Cora and earth magic. You'll attend two elemental lessons every day for three hours each."

"Three hours? That's twice as long as my classes last year."

"We decided longer classes would allow us to approach your training with more depth. I'm super excited to work directly with you and I'm sure the others are as well. Angeline has had you all to herself for too long."

Conryu found the idea of studying with such powerful and experienced wizards surprisingly exciting. "When do we start?"

"You and me, first thing Monday morning." She giggled. "I pulled rank to get my hands on you first. Anything you're particularly eager to learn?"

"I want to fly."

Her eyes lit up. "I love flying. I can't wait to see how fast you can go. This will be so great."

Conryu's excitement dimmed. "What about Anya? How am I supposed to protect her and attend class?"

"Her teachers will be responsible for her safety during the day. You only have to escort her to and from class and the dorm and be ready to act at night." Another giggle. "I imagine having a girl like that next door keeps you plenty ready at night."

Conryu sighed. "Don't say things like that. Maria's already upset with the situation."

"Don't worry. Once you settle into a regular routine, everyone will forget all about it."

Conryu thought about the gorgeous girl outside and seriously doubted anyone would forget about her living next door to him.

"Oh, yeah. I assume you know Angus won't be joining us this semester?"

He brightened. "I did. It seems his unauthorized biography is doing well, so the publisher sent him on a book tour. *Merlin Reborn*, what a joke. He didn't even offer to cut me in for a percentage. Since it's my life he's writing about you'd think I'd get something."

"You did," Dean Blane said. "Half a year with no Professor."

* * *

Anya paced and watched as Conryu helped set up tables for the welcome ceremony tonight. He'd volunteered to help a crew of twenty girls get the cafeteria ready for the celebration. She didn't know what to do with herself. Everyone seemed so relaxed here. It was weird. The rest of the freshmen were due to arrive in a few hours. The smells coming from the kitchen made her twisty stomach churn.

The plan was for her to slip into the flow of new arrivals and mix in like she'd just arrived on the train. It seemed like a perfect time for the czar's agents to grab her, but the teachers all assured her they'd be on full alert. Besides, the odds of someone plucking her out of a group of hundreds of girls and getting away was beyond remote. If the czar wanted to kill her, on the other hand, the chances grew much better.

She jumped when one of the tables screeched as Conryu pushed it into place. He offered a reassuring smile. Maybe it was stupid to be so on edge here, but after everything that had happened she didn't dare drop her guard, even with Conryu nearby.

Anya turned on her heel and found his flying book a foot from her face. "Gah!" She leapt back, her heart racing.

"Too much anxiety isn't good for humans," the book said.

"You floating a foot from my face isn't helping my anxiety any." Anya took a deep breath and tried to relax. The book had a point. Getting herself worked up wasn't going to help anything.

"Prime!" She turned to find Conryu looking at her, or more precisely, at his book. "Behave yourself."

"I was offering your new female words of comfort. She seemed uneasy."

"For the last time, she is not my female. And having been under threat of death myself a few times I can tell you anxiety is totally natural. Now stop pestering her."

"Yes, Master." The book, Prime, flew over closer to its master.

Anya sighed. Maybe a project would take her mind off

things. She went to join Conryu who had moved on to lining up chairs. "What can I do?"

"You can lay out the plates. Don't mind Prime. He has the manners of a demon."

"I am a demon," Prime said.

Conryu grinned and she felt some of the weight lift off her shoulders. He was a nice guy and he seemed to want to do his best to keep her safe. That was something.

She set a plate in front of the first chair. "Can you run me through the ceremony?" Avoiding surprises would help her relax, maybe.

"It's not really a big deal. The freshmen will file in and you'll approach the testing device which tells you your elemental alignment. Try to act surprised when you touch the earth gem. Once everyone's done we have a big meal and go to bed to sleep it off."

"Sounds simple enough." Conryu's friend Kelsie had wandered up to lay out silverware. The girl offered her a shy smile which Anya returned.

"Yeah, nothing to it. Tomorrow you'll have your Awakening then go to your first class. The teachers will protect you until lunch when I take over. I suspect that pattern will hold until midterms after which we head home for winter break. Speaking of winter break, are you crashing at my place again?"

"I assume so, though I would like to visit my mom."

"Do vampires celebrate Christmas?" Conryu asked.

The laugh slipped past her lips before she realized it was coming. How long had it been since she really laughed? It felt like forever. "We don't even celebrate it in the Empire. We have a midwinter carnival. There's ice skating, spiced cider, roasted chestnuts, and a dance. Our schools teach that Christmas is a decadent excuse to waste money on junk."

"Sounds about right." Conryu looked past her. "What do you think about an air mattress?"

"What?" Kelsie seemed caught off guard by the question. Anya was as well, come to that.

"I thought if we got you an air mattress you wouldn't need to stay with Maria during winter break. Would that work?"

"I guess."

Anya suppressed a smile at Kelsie's blush. He really was a nice guy.

* * *

M aria sat beside Conryu as they waited for the freshmen to enter the cafeteria. The lights were down and the testing device in place. She'd kept a close eye on him and Anya during the preparations and while they'd been friendly, she couldn't find a thing wrong with their behavior. After the fool she made of herself last year over Kelsie, Maria didn't plan to overreact this year. Still, it seemed impossible that he'd ended up living in such close proximity to another beautiful girl. There had to be some plain wizards needing protection.

Kelsie sat on the other side of Conryu and the two of them were discussing air mattresses of all things. She wasn't sure if she wanted to know what that was about. To her left and right girls chattered about the coming year and what new spells they might learn.

"So do you know what you're studying this year?" Conryu's question caught her by surprise. Her mind had been wandering and she didn't even notice when he stopped talking to Kelsie.

"The basics of the four physical elements and advanced light magic. What about you?"

He glanced around as though checking to see if anyone was listening. "I'm studying one on one with the department heads. Dean Blane is going to teach me to fly. How cool is that?"

Maria nearly choked. The department heads were going to train him themselves? "Why?"

"She asked me what I wanted to learn and I thought it would be fun to fly, like riding my bike, but without the bike."

"No, why are you studying with the department heads?"

"Oh, according to Dean Blane I did so well with Mrs. Umbra that she decided to extend my arrangement to the other elements. Sounds like everyone is pretty stoked to see what I can do. I'm just glad I won't have to spend hours every week on something I could learn in an afternoon. It got kind of tedious last year."

Before Maria had a chance to dive into a tirade about learning things in the proper order, the back door opened and the freshmen filed in. It didn't take long to spot Anya. Maria couldn't remember meeting anyone as attractive as that girl.

A line formed in front of the tester and one after another the new arrivals found out their aligned element. The hall got a good shaking when Anya touched the earth gem. She was strong, no doubt about that.

When she finished Anya joined them at their table and Conryu pulled her chair out for her.

"No problems?" he asked.

"No, everyone was very nice, and Mrs. Saint stayed close by just in case."

"Told you. I suppose it was a little anticlimactic since you already knew your aligned element."

"Not at all," Anya said. "When I touched the gem at the Ministry, the room didn't shake like that. I was quite startled."

"You should have been here last year," Kelsie said. "When Conryu touched the black gem, it was like the whole room plunged into Hell. There were red eyes everywhere and the temperature must have dropped twenty degrees."

"Creepy." Anya shivered.

Conryu grinned. "You think that was bad, you should have seen what happened at my Awakening."

The door to the kitchen opened and platters of food flew out sparing Maria from having to relive that nightmare. Dinner only lasted an hour or so this year and the next thing she knew Maria was in bed staring at the ceiling.

Tomorrow was her first day of classes and that usually left her excited, but tonight she couldn't stop thinking about Conryu studying with the department heads. He'd already pulled so far ahead of her. At this rate she'd never catch up.

* * *

Yarik gaped like a junior agent making his first visit to the Imperial Palace. Central City sprawled in front of him as he drove down the highway. Massive skyscrapers filled the skyline, taller than anything in New St. Petersburg by a tremendous margin. They'd been driving for a day and a half almost nonstop since acquiring the truck and now they'd almost reached their destination.

Ahead of them a sign indicated a rest area approached, half a mile up the highway. Yarik signaled then pulled off and parked.

"Why are we stopping?" Victor asked.

"I need to figure out where we have to go. If possible, I'd

just as soon avoid the city. It's the nation's capital and there are bound to be wizards everywhere. Should one of them notice you two and figure out what you are we'll be in trouble."

Hedon snorted. "We can kill any wizard that sees us."

Yarik slapped his forehead. "There are probably dozens if not hundreds of wizards in a city that big. I have great respect for your abilities, but I'm not sure the two of you taking on an entire city is a good bet."

He dug out his phone and called up the map again. The academy wasn't actually in the city which worked out well for them. In fact, it sat in the middle of a forest fifty miles northwest. On the downside, the only way to reach it, other than hiking, was by train. Since they couldn't sneak aboard a train, they'd have to go on foot.

He closed the map and pulled up a text editor that contained numerous facts about the area. It also held the name of an Imperial spy working deep cover in Central. Much as he hated having to go into the city, Yarik needed to get in touch and see what information she had. According to the file the best place to make contact was a tattoo parlor in a rough part of town known as The Bleakes. Hopefully avoiding the city center would reduce their chances of running into any wizards.

"We're going in. Keep your powers fully suppressed just to be safe."

Yarik fired up the pickup and pulled back onto the highway. They had the modest good fortune that the area where the spy lived was on this side of the city, so they didn't have to drive all the way around.

Half an hour later Yarik was weaving his way down crowded city streets. Cars lined both sides of the road, sometimes narrowing it down so only a single vehicle could fit through. Horns honked and drivers swore. It seemed so chaotic after the Empire. Yarik hadn't seen a single checkpoint. How did the rulers of this country keep track of who went where? Not that the Empire did such a great job in that regard, but at least they made the effort.

Three streets to go until they reached the tattoo parlor. The only authority he'd seen so far was a single city guardsman in a blue uniform and he just walked along on the sidewalk, pausing to occasionally speak to one of the locals. No one even fled in fear when they saw him. He must not have much power.

"Agent, to your right," Victor said.

Yarik spotted the stylized dragon over the door of the tattoo parlor. That had to be the one he wanted. Half a block up he pulled into a parking spot and the three of them got out.

"Victor, remain with the truck. The last thing we need is for someone to steal it. Hedon, you're with me."

They made the short walk back to the tattoo parlor and Yarik pulled the door open. Every sort of image you could think of decorated the shop walls. Two chairs sat in the middle of the main room and a beaded curtain blocked a doorway he assumed led to an office. Behind the counter a fat man in a leather vest eyed them through lowered sunglasses. Every inch of his skin looked like an advertisement for his services. Of the female spy he saw no sign.

"Help you two?" the fat man asked.

"We're looking for Iris. Word is she does the best dragon tattoos in the city."

"I do a mean dragon myself." The fat man twisted his arm to show them a green, fire-breathing monster on his tricep. "Maybe I can do what you need."

"Your work is excellent," Yarik said. "However, we had our minds made up that we wanted silver-scaled dragons."

The artist grimaced. "She'd never let me use one of her exclusive designs. Yo, Iris! You got customers."

A dark-haired woman in a gypsy skirt and red shirt pushed through the curtain. She had a dragon decorating her face from chin to eyebrow. From the color of her hair and shape of her nose Yarik pegged her as coming from the southern part of the Empire.

"Can't I even eat lunch in peace, Piers?" Iris asked.

The fat man shrugged. "They asked for a silver dragon. Unless you want to pass up the payday..."

She eyed Yarik more closely. "No, that's okay. Step back into the office and I'll show you boys some samples."

"Thank you." Yarik and Hedon followed her through the curtain and into a simple office. Art books covered a rusty steel table.

Iris opened one of them and every page had a different dragon design. "Which one do you like?"

Yarik flipped through until he found an exact duplicate to the Imperial seal. "I believe this one will suit me perfectly."

"A fine choice. Unfortunately, I'm out of the ink I need to do that design. Perhaps a rain check?"

"That's disappointing, but very well."

She wrote a note on a small slip of paper. "Excellent, it shouldn't be more than a day or two."

Yarik accepted the paper and nodded. She escorted him and Hedon to the door and saw them off. When they were outside Hedon said, "Must we wait two days?"

"No." Yarik led the way back to the truck. "This isn't a rain check, it's an address with 'eight o'clock' next to it. We'll get what we need tonight and be on our way tomorrow."

4

UNWELCOME GUESTS

G eneral Ivan stood in the front of the bobbing cargo ship that had carried them to Constanta and stared through the thick fog at the barely visible warehouses beyond the docks. The empty hulk of a coast guard cutter floated at one of the piers. The unfortunate sailors had been killed about a month ago while pursuing the czar's runaway witch. An appalling waste of Imperial assets.

On either side of his ship, two coast guard cutters, perfect twins to the empty one ahead, awaited his orders. The plan was to level the warehouses and destroy any vampires inside before beginning construction on the prefab fortification crowding the ship's deck.

Ivan took a deep breath of heavy, briny air and grimaced at the rotten-fish stink that permeated everything. The empty city didn't even have an active fishing fleet, yet the docks still stank. It almost felt like magic, a curse of some sort.

He shook off the distracting thoughts. If he failed to complete the mission, his life was forfeit, he understood that.

No one that served in the czar's court for any length of time held any illusions about their master's patience. What the czar wanted he got and if you couldn't get it for him he'd find someone that could.

He'd just begun to wonder where all the birds were when Nosorova marched up to join him. The witch made him nervous. She didn't fit neatly into his chain of command and anything that didn't fit was suspect in Ivan's eyes. That said, he wouldn't have wanted to attempt this mission without a witch or preferably, several witches, with him.

"Are you planning to stare at it all day or are we going to get started?" Nosorova asked. "Daylight is burning and I'll need every bit of it to lay out the ward."

"I was simply getting a feel for the land to determine the best place to construct our fort."

"You were delaying the inevitable." Nosorova spoke without any hint of caring about his precarious position. And why should she? The witches were, and always had been, the czar's favorites.

Ivan unclipped a radio from his belt. "Begin bombardment."

The cannons of first one then the other cutter boomed. The shells struck a direct hit to one of the warehouses, blowing it sky high. No turning back now. Shots had been fired. They were at war.

The flames of the explosion gave him a better look at the docks. There was a wide flat area twenty yards from the water. That would be a perfect place to build and they wouldn't have to carry the panels far.

The attacks continued until there wasn't a place standing big enough to hide a mouse, much less a vampire. The cargo ship advanced as close to shore as possible. Crewmen ran to throw lines. Ivan stood and watched, the silent witch beside him.

When they were secured to the dock Ivan asked, "Do you need anything from me to set your protections in place?"

"All I need is to know where and how large to make the barrier. The sooner the better as it will take hours to fully erect."

Ivan pointed to the flat spot he'd noted earlier. "Right there. The outer wall will enclose a space forty yards on each side."

"I'll enclose a forty-five-yards square, just to be safe. Give me an hour to set the outermost line before you begin unloading." The witch muttered something and flew toward shore.

Ivan silently cursed the woman. How dare she give orders to a general? But who was he kidding? Of the two of them, he was by far the more expendable.

The ship's captain strode up to him, his white uniform gleaming in the sun. "Shall we get started, sir?"

"Give her an hour to prepare the area." Ivan choked the words out.

Down on shore, Nosorova paced and wove her hands through intricate passes. Ivan couldn't make out what she said, but he assumed it was a spell since every few seconds a golden spark leapt from her hand and struck the ground.

Just shy of an hour later the witch flew into the air and hovered above the construction site. Since she'd moved out of the way he took it as a sign that they could begin working. He gave the signal and the engineers and their teams got started. Cranes raised and lowered massive sections of steel wall while the welders and construction workers put them together. It was an amazing process.

Near dusk, heavy sodium lights flicked on, illuminating the project. The walls were mostly up, but they hadn't started on the actual fortress yet. At last Nosorova landed beside him at the front of the ship.

"It's done." She looked like she'd climbed a mountain without oxygen. "We have fifteen minutes until sunset. Everyone needs to be inside the wards before then."

"Including the ships' crews?"

Nosorova looked at him with shadowed eyes. "Anyone you still want breathing in the morning."

Ivan stared for a moment then decided she meant it. He barked orders into his radio. If anything happened to his workers, he wouldn't be able to finish the project without returning to the Empire for help. He shuddered to think what the czar might do to him.

In the end they got everyone inside with two minutes to spare. He'd ordered the lights on the ship left on so they wouldn't be fully in the dark.

The workers had erected a single watchtower and Ivan climbed it along with the witch. He doubted it would take long to discover the efficacy of her wards. If they failed, no one would survive long enough to complain.

"They're here," Nosorova said.

Ivan squinted in the dark. A moment later the first dark figure seemed to materialize out of the night. He'd never seen a vampire in person. They didn't look terribly impressive. Pale figures that seemed to waver, one moment solid and the next mist. One of them, a woman he thought, reached a hand out.

Golden light sparked and she yanked it back.

"It seems your wards are effective," Ivan said. "Congratulations."

"Don't congratulate me yet, the enemy still hasn't tested them."

At first Ivan didn't understand, then four of the vampires

gathered in a circle. A sphere of darkness formed between them and they hurled it at the fort. He flinched when a web of golden light flashed into being, but it didn't break.

Thrice more the vampires tested the fortress's defenses and thrice more they held. Soon enough the vampires faded back into the darkness. It seemed they would survive the first night at least.

* * *

Following the directions provided by his cell phone— Yarik had to admit the electronics available to people outside the Empire certainly put anything they had to shame— he and the dragon-bloods reached a rundown tenement where Iris said to meet her. Looking around the wretched neighborhood Yarik was reminded of home for the first time since falling out of the portal. It made him feel oddly better to know this place of such wealth still had sections of squalor. He preferred not to think about what that said about his twisted psyche.

They got out of the truck and this time Hedon stayed behind. In a place like this Yarik doubted they'd have a vehicle to return to if no one guarded it. A quick scan of the area revealed no threats to Yarik's limited vision, but given Victor's calm stride he felt comfortable enough in his analysis.

They marched down the sidewalk to the building's front door. The moment Yarik pushed it open the stink of garbage and shit washed over him. Swallowing his gorge, Yarik headed for the stairs. The meeting was set for an apartment on the third floor. The sooner they got it over with the better.

Rusty iron steps creaked and crunched under Victor's weight, but they reached the third landing without crashing through. The apartment they wanted was only a few steps from the door. Yarik knocked and a moment later the door opened revealing Iris's face.

"You're punctual, I'll give you that." The door closed and the safety chain slid out. When the door opened again Iris waved them inside. The interior matched the rest of the building, but she had something burning that covered the stink.

"You couldn't find a nicer place?" Yarik asked.

"I don't live here. This unit is strictly for quiet meetings. The people living here don't care about anything beyond their next high. I find that indifference useful. Now, what can I do for you, Agent?"

"How did you know I was an agent?"

She snorted a laugh. "I met enough of you before I left to recognize your type."

"I didn't think I was so obvious. Anyway, my mission is to retrieve a girl from the magic school. I hoped you might have some information on the best ways in and out. From the little I've seen it looks pretty isolated."

Iris shook her head. "You've been given a fool's errand. You'll never get past the wizards, even if you have a dragon-blood to help you."

"We have other items at our disposal to distract the wizards. I'm confident we can grab the girl, it's escaping with her that's the problem. There's nowhere for a car to approach."

"No, the only nonmagical form of transportation is the train. If you want any hope of escaping, you'll need to strike when it's there unloading supplies. You can force the conductor to bring you to the city where a car will be waiting."

"That might work. I don't suppose you know the train's delivery schedule?"

"In point of fact I do." Iris went into the apartment's small bedroom and emerged a few seconds later with a battered notebook. She flipped it open and thumbed through the pages. "Here we go. Supplies go in at midmorning on Sunday, every week, like clockwork. That's when you strike."

Yarik frowned. Assuming they set out tomorrow it would take at least two days to hike in. It was Monday, so that left two days to study the layout of the campus and get a feel for the students' movements. It would be tight, but doable.

"I appreciate your help, but I wonder how it is that you had just the information I needed."

"That's my job, Agent. The first thing I researched upon arriving was how best to take down the academy. I concluded it wasn't possible short of a full invasion. I wish you the best of luck."

Yarik nodded his thanks. After listening to Iris he suspected they'd need all the luck they could get.

* * *

Conryu climbed the steps to the roof on his way to his first class with Dean Blane, Prime floating along beside him. He'd said he wanted to learn to fly, so she told him to meet her on the roof. Nerves warred with excitement as he climbed. After her Awakening, which had thankfully gone off without a hitch, Conryu dropped Anya off at her basic earth magic class. Before lunch he was supposed to bring her to the nurse's office for another blood test, but between then and now he didn't have to worry about her.

It wasn't that Conryu didn't like Anya or want to keep her safe; it was just that he saw no sign of danger. She'd been in the Alliance for five days now and no one had taken a shot at her. He hoped the Empire had given up and moved on to terrorizing other people. If they had given up, how long was he going to have to look after her? Maybe if nothing happened, they'd let him off the hook after midterms. Hopefully. It wasn't like she could live with him for the rest of her life.

He shook his head and opened the roof access door. If you were going to learn to fly, this was a perfect day for it. The sun shone bright overhead; it was about seventy-five degrees, and the wind calm. Near the edge of the roof Dean Blane stood waiting, her pale-blue robe flapping in the breeze.

She beamed when Conryu shut the door behind him. "Excited? I know I am."

"Yeah, nervous too. I've never done anything but universal and dark spells. Do you think I'll have any trouble with wind magic?"

"I can't imagine you would. The wind gem reacted to you, so technically you're wind aligned as well. The only way to know for sure is to give it a shot."

Conryu nodded and joined her at the edge of the roof. It looked a lot higher now that he was about to jump off.

"The spell is pretty simple. It translates to, 'Father of winds, carry me into your domain. Air Rider.' It sounds much different in the language of elemental air." Dean Blane made a series of whistles and hisses. When she stopped, she was floating. "Nothing to it. Remember, like all magic, your will controls your reality. You need to concentrate to get the spirits to do what you want."

Conryu nodded. The language of air was even more alien than the guttural sounds of Infernal. It reminded him a bit of a bird and a snake having a conversation. Conryu cleared his mind and focused. He pictured himself floating beside Dean Blane and copied the sounds she made earlier. Nothing happened.

"That was close," she said. "But you mispronounced the last word. It's 'rider' not 'raider.'"

She corrected his pronunciation and Conryu took a breath. "Father of winds, carry me into your domain. Air Rider."

Power gathered around him and he was up. Conryu spun in a circle then flipped upside down, his robe falling in his face. Dean Blane giggled.

"Focus, Master. Your mind is all over the place."

Conryu scowled and righted himself. When he could see again, he found the roof thirty feet below him. His eyes bulged and he nearly lost it for a second time. He caught the stray thought before it could upend him again.

"You're doing great." Dean Blane flew in a little circle around him. "It usually takes weeks before a student gets off the ground. Want to try a few maneuvers?"

"Sure."

She paused right in front of him. "Just copy me."

Dean Blane glided left and Conryu mirrored her.

"No, Master, don't think, 'do what she does,' think, 'glide left.' You need to be able to do this yourself when there's no one to copy."

Conryu shot Prime a look. "How do you fly? You can't even use wind magic, can you?"

"No," Prime said. "I use dark magic to negate the effects of gravity. It's a demon thing, humans can't do it."

"Why not?" If he could fly with dark magic, it would be much easier than learning a whole other type of spell.

"Demons resonate with this reality differently than humans," Dean Blane said. "They're less bound by its rules."

"Oh, bummer."

They spent the next hour going through basic movements until Conryu had mastered moving up and down and side to side. He couldn't stop grinning as they looped around the roof. It almost felt like a dance.

"You're a natural," Dean Blane said. "Are you getting tired yet?"

"No, this spell doesn't draw much power from me."

She smiled and shook her head. "Want to try something a little faster?"

His grin broadened. If there was one thing Conryu loved, it was going fast. "Hell, yeah. What did you have in mind?"

"A race across the lake. Just give it all you've got."

"Cool. Will you be able to keep up okay, Prime?"

"Don't worry, Master, I'll be pulled along by our link. Have no fear of us being separated."

Conryu turned to Dean Blane. "On three?"

She grinned back at him like a little girl about to get into mischief. "One."

"Two," he said.

"Three!"

She darted ahead, blasting across the water a few feet above the surface. Conryu took off after her. All his will focused on powering forward.

Halfway across he was only a body length behind her.

Faster!

A quarter length between them now.

Faster!!

He shot past her and a loud boom followed. The trees on the far side grew really big really fast. He pulled up as hard as he could, but still crashed through the small branches at the top.

Conryu slowed and stopped far above the forest. He gasped for air like he'd run a hundred-yard dash. What a rush! That made his bike seem like riding a turtle.

Dean Blane flew up beside him, her hair plastered to her face. "That was impressive. I didn't think you'd pass me on your first try. I didn't think you'd break the sound barrier either. Be careful not to go that fast near the school, you'll shatter our windows."

"Did I really break the sound barrier?"

She nodded. "You couldn't see it, but you had a huge tornado pushing you forward. Now that I've seen you, I'd say your power level in wind is about fifteen thousand."

Nine thousand less than his dark magic level. He hadn't thought the drop off would be that much. "Is that good?"

"Are you kidding? It's over twice my strength and I'm the most powerful wind wizard in the Alliance. If you wanted to I bet you could conjure an F5 tornado. We're not going to try that today."

"Yeah, better save that for next week. Oh, shit! Prime, what time is it?"

"Almost eleven, Master."

"Damn it! I'm going to be late meeting Anya."

* * *

Conryu finished his lunch, dropped Anya off at History of Magic, and turned toward Mrs. Umbra's office. She hadn't said what they were going to work on this year. In truth, there wasn't much about dark magic Prime couldn't teach him. Not that he didn't think Mrs. Umbra had a lot to offer, it just struck him that of all the elements, dark offered him the easiest path forward.

The scholomantic flew a little behind him, his nervousness coming through their link. No matter how many times Conryu tried to reassure Prime that the Head of Dark Magic wasn't so bad, he refused to believe it. Who would have imagined a scaredy-cat demon?

It didn't take long to make the walk to the administrative area. The secretaries had seen enough of him by this point that they hardly even blinked as he walked past. Mrs. Umbra's office wasn't that far from Dean Blane's.

Conryu rapped on her door and a muffled voice said, "Come in."

He pushed through and found Mrs. Umbra standing in front of her desk, arms crossed, her frown making her many wrinkles look even deeper. What could she be upset about? It was still the first day of class for goodness' sake.

"Let me see it."

He blinked. "Excuse me?"

"The Reaper's Mark. Show it to me."

Conryu rolled up his sleeve and held out his marked arm. She stalked over, grabbed his wrist, and made a pass over the scythe.

Mrs. Umbra jerked her hand back and shook it. "It's a powerful connection. There's no way you'll be able to remove the mark by compelling the Reaper, even with the Death Stick. What were you thinking?"

He pushed his sleeve back down. "Reaper's Cloak was the only spell that would allow me to close the portals and save the city. How was I supposed to know the cloak's owner would show up and pretend to slice my arm off? I'm not thrilled with the situation, but I can't see anything I might have done differently besides letting Sentinel City get torn apart by shadow beasts."

For a moment she looked exhausted, but the moment passed quickly. Mrs. Umbra retreated around her desk and nodded toward the guest chairs. Conryu sat and waited while she rubbed her eyes. He hated causing her stress, but then there was nothing he could do about what had happened.

At last she looked up. "I assume you have no idea what getting marked by the Reaper means."

"I figured it worked the same way as my other brands, not that he seemed to need a power boost. My big hope is that a connection to the Reaper will keep the other demons a safe distance away." Probably best not to mention his potential company of ninjas.

She barked a laugh. "Hardly. There's a class of magic within the dark element that is directly associated with death. Reaper's Cloak, Reaper's Gale, Dread Scythe, and a number of others. For someone with a mark like yours, all those spells will have a greater effect than ordinary. Given your base power, you must be even more careful when casting them."

"Reaper's Cloak seemed strictly defensive."

"For anyone else it would be, but with your connection you can wield a portion of Death's power directly while wearing it. You must have seen the souls of others when you used the spell."

He'd never forget those flickering ghost flames and the cold voice telling him how simple it would be to snuff them out. "I didn't realize the spell allowed that. I figured he was trying to tempt me into doing something I shouldn't."

"That's part of it as well. Since I heard what happened, I've spoken with some of my contacts in Hell. No one has any idea what the Reaper has planned for you. I find that most alarming."

"You and me both. So what are we going to do?"

"I don't know that there's anything we can do. The Reaper is the most powerful demon in existence. That said, there's one thing you can't forget. For all his power, the Reaper can't force you to do anything you don't want to do. As long as you can resist the temptation to use his power, you're safe from him. Or as safe as anyone is from Death."

* * *

General Ivan studied the rapidly rising fortress and smiled. The outer wall enclosed ninety percent of the perimeter, and most of the first floor of the main building had been built. In another two, maybe three days, they'd have an unassailable foothold in the enemy's territory. The czar would be very pleased and the best part was the vampires were helpless to do anything about it thanks to Nosorova's ward.

He had to admit he'd held doubts about her ability to keep the undead out, but she'd proven him wrong. And thank goodness for that. If the monsters had somehow broken through... Ivan shuddered. Best not to think about that.

The crew only had another hour or so of daylight to work. Despite the lights from the ship, it was safer for everyone if they stopped at night. The construction needed to be done right. He had no desire to risk his life in a shoddily built fort.

Far above him the white-robed form of the witch floated. She'd been up there since right after breakfast and she didn't land for lunch. Whatever the woman was working on must have been important. Ivan hated to admit ignorance about anything, but when it came to magic, he didn't have a clue.

As the sun sank behind the mountains, Nosorova finally landed. She wobbled a bit when her feet touched the ground, the first sign of weakness he'd seen from her. Nice to know that despite her powers she was still human.

"Is all well?" Ivan asked.

She nodded. "The wards are as powerful as I can make

them. All I need is to tie them to the fortress and they'll be complete."

Nosorova strode past him toward the partially complete building and Ivan followed, curious to see what she'd do next.

The interior of the fort didn't even have dividing walls yet, but she made straight for the center of the building. On the plans there was a pillar in the main gathering area that served no structural purpose. That must be what she wanted.

Sure enough, Nosorova paused in front of a smooth stone cylinder and placed her hands on it. Energy flowed and crackled up its length. Lines like lightning streamed in and struck the pillar. One of them passed through Ivan, but he felt nothing.

He couldn't stop staring as more and more strands came flying in. Nosorova wove them together and through the pillar. After he knew not how long, the magic vanished and she slumped in obvious exhaustion.

"It's done. The wards are now permanent and linked to this structure."

"What does that mean for us?" Ivan asked.

"It means that as long as the keystone remains unharmed the wards will continue to function. I need to return to the Empire. So much distance between me and the czar has left me weak."

Ivan made a dismissive gesture. They were safe from the vampires and that was all that mattered.

Nosorova chanted and vanished in a gust of wind, leaving him alone in the chamber. Good riddance to the witch. With her gone he wouldn't need to share his success. Oh, he'd praise her hard work, the czar would appreciate that, but he'd be sure to emphasize his leadership in guiding the affair. He smiled and walked back into the yard.

WRATH OF THE DRAGON CZAR

The sun had almost set. Time to head up to the watchtower so he could see the monsters flail against his impenetrable defenses.

As if summoned by his thought, a group of six vampires appeared out of the near-perpetual fog. They dragged their claws across the invisible barrier, drawing golden sparks, but seeming to do no harm. The monsters snarled and bared their fangs, like the stupid animals they were.

It struck him as unfair that the others couldn't watch the show. He whistled and waved to draw the soldiers' attention. "Come take a look!"

One of the men got the bright idea to drive a scissor lift beside the wall. They piled onto the platform and raised it up so they could see over the top. They were soon all laughing and jeering at the vampires who glared back with glowing red eyes.

Ivan couldn't help watching with a bright smile. This was exactly what the men needed, to see the enemy wasn't invincible. It would give them confidence in the coming battles.

A few minutes later everyone had gathered on whatever piece of equipment they could find. A couple even brought rifles and took a few pot shots at the assembled vampires. Ivan should have warned them not to waste their ammo, but they had plenty and it was a bit of harmless fun. His men had been working hard, they deserved to blow off a little steam.

* * *

In the absolute darkness of his portable sleep chamber, Talon felt the witch's powerful presence vanish. Minutes remained before the setting sun freed him from his daily rest.

With her gone he had no hesitation about dealing with Roman's lackeys.

The wards she created were powerful enough to keep even him out, but he had a simple way around that. She constructed them specifically to stop his kind, but a normal, living human could enter and leave at will. He had many loyal humans living in his lands and none of them had any desire for Roman to take over their country. The moment he recognized how the protections worked, Talon had summoned one of his most talented servants.

The sun sank below the horizon, taking with it the paralysis that held him. Transforming into black mist, he exited his sleep chamber. He'd taken up position a quarter mile from Constanta on a little-used side road. Outside his limousine a single man took a knee as he re-formed. A lean, fit human of thirty years, Xavier Lancer was Talon's finest agent and perfect for completing the task at hand.

"Command me, my lord," Xavier said, head bowed.

"You've seen the affront polluting our lands?"

"Yes, Lord Talon. I observed the fort for several hours this afternoon. The soldiers are overconfident and keep a poor guard. Their numbers are all that give me pause."

"You need not fight them, Xavier, simply open the path for us." Talon reached into the folds of his jacket and emerged with a shiny black sphere the size of a large marble. "Take this and shatter it against the ward focus."

"How will I know it, my lord?"

"Do you recall when I sent you to spy on that cult that set up shop in the ruins of Prague?"

Xavier nodded.

"I will meld minds with you again so I can see what you see. I'll know the focus when I see it and I'll point it out to you."

"Understood." Xavier took the sphere and slipped it into his pocket. "Shall I go now?"

"Not just yet. The others will put on a show for the foolish Imperials. Get closer, but wait until I give you the signal to begin your infiltration."

Talon reached out and placed a hand on either side of Xavier's head. Immortal crimson eyes locked with ice-blue human ones. It took only moments to link their minds. All of Xavier's knowledge and secrets were his to explore, every sense his to use. Out of respect for his loyal servant, Talon didn't probe too deep.

Talon blinked and returned his focus to his own body. "It's done. Go now and wait for my command."

Xavier vanished into the fog as silent as a vampire. It wouldn't take the agile human long to get in position. Talon shifted his focus to the others. He'd brought half a dozen of his most skilled warriors on this mission.

He sent his thoughts outward toward where the others capered and snarled for the humans.

Marek, how goes the distraction?

More of the fools gather by the second. Give them two more minutes and every so-called guard will be watching us.

Talon shifted his focus back to Xavier. His agent crouched in the ruins of one of the destroyed warehouses across from the fort. His vision seemed far too feeble to Talon, but then again he was only human.

Two minutes passed.

Go.

No hesitation from Xavier as he sprinted straight across the open space separating his hiding spot from the fort. He pressed himself tight to the wall. Talon felt the pounding of his heart and smiled in the dark. It had been seventeen centuries since his heart beat its last. Sharing minds with a human was worth it for that long-forgotten sensation alone.

Xavier eased along toward the unfinished section, straining with his meager senses to detect any threat. How did humans survive with such limited awareness of the world?

A shadow passed in front of the open section. Xavier ducked out of sight and held his breath.

No reaction. The guard hadn't spotted him.

Perhaps the feeble senses of humans weren't such a bad thing after all.

Xavier continued his painfully slow approach. At the edge of the opening he peeked inside. A single guard stood with his back to the gap. He wore the white uniform of the Imperial army. A rifle hung from his shoulder and a knife was belted at his hip.

Inch by inch, Xavier eased closer. When only a foot separated them he lunged, wrapping his forearm around the guard's throat. The enemy struggled for a few seconds then went still.

A tickle in the back of his mind distracted Talon. He disengaged from his agent and focused on it. *Marek?*

The humans are getting bored, Talon. You need to hurry.

Talon shifted his focus back to Xavier and sent feelings of urgency through the link. Dead ahead of him was the partially constructed fort. Even from a distance Talon sensed the key stone. No guards protected the structure so Xavier sprinted over and through the rough door.

Inside the only item of note was a central column. It seethed with magic.

That's it, Xavier. Throw the sphere against the column.

Talon felt the acknowledgement and Xavier dug the sphere out of his pocket.

"Hey, you there. What are you doing?" One of the soldiers at the edge of the gathering had noticed Xavier.

Hurry.

Xavier hurled the sphere.

It struck home and shattered.

Bullets pinged all around him.

Xavier leapt behind a wall as dark energy burst from the broken sphere and erased the wards.

Talon withdrew from his agent's mind.

Attack!

Following his own command, Talon raced toward the fort. He moved at speeds no human could hope to match. In seconds he reached the wall and leapt over it.

Marek and the others were already busy slaughtering the soldiers. He sensed no pain from Xavier and the man knew enough to keep out of the way when the vampires were in a frenzy.

Content to let his people deal with the soldiers, Talon swept the area in search of the enemy commander. He spotted the man cowering in the watchtower.

Talon turned into mist, flew up beside him, and solidified. The human's terror excited him. Talon's fangs extended to their full four-inch length.

"Please don't kill me. Please don't kill me." The general gibbered and begged.

Satisfying as it would have been to tear the coward's throat out and bathe in his blood, someone needed to carry Talon's message back to Roman.

He reached out, grabbed the general by the throat, and lifted him off the floor. The stink of urine turned Talon's stomach.

"Look close, Imperial, and see what happens to those that

try to invade my domain." Talon forced the general to watch as the others slaughtered his men without mercy.

The soldiers' guns were useless and they were so afraid they missed most of their shots anyway. The battle, if you wanted to call it that, ended in minutes. When the last soldier was dead Talon hurled the general off the watchtower. The human landed with a grunt of pain.

Talon materialized beside him. "I'm going to spare your useless life. In exchange for my generosity you will take this message to Roman. His empire isn't welcome here and anyone that crosses the border without my permission will face the same fate as your men. Do you understand?"

The general nodded as tears streamed down his face.

"Someone put this wretch on a boat and get him on his way. The sight of him sickens me."

A vampire led the general away. Hopefully Roman would take the hint and let this matter drop. If he didn't, well, his people seldom dined on human blood. If the Imperials wanted to provide them a feast, they wouldn't turn it down.

* * *

Conryu took his time climbing the stairs to the light magic floor. St. Seraphim said she wanted to meet him there instead of in her office. So far he'd had one class with all the department heads but her and this was the one that had him the most worried. Conryu's strongest aptitude was in dark magic so he had no idea how he'd do with light. Dean Blane assured him that he had a modest alignment with light magic and that even if he didn't, his raw power would still give him a well-above-average chance to succeed in the field.

Maybe Prime's bad vibes passing through their link had

him on edge. Ever since the scholomantic learned he'd be studying light magic he'd been trying to convince Conryu not to do it. Prime worried about the magic traveling through their link and hurting him. That didn't strike Conryu as very likely, but then he didn't really know much about it.

Conryu stepped into the hall and checked the nearest door. It was labeled seven. St. Seraphim said to meet her in room three. He shrugged and turned right. The floor wasn't that big, he'd find the right room soon enough.

"If you can't find it, Master, we can still call the whole thing off."

"Don't be such a wimp, Prime. If I'd known light magic healing I could have saved Jonny a lot of recovery time. I'm going to make this work and you're going to help me."

"I know almost nothing about light magic. All demons care about is how to kill those who wield it."

"I'll be wielding it shortly, so you'd best get used to the idea. Here it is."

The door to room three was partway open. Taking that as an invitation he pushed through. Twenty desks faced a blackboard. A bookcase covered one wall. No sign of a teacher.

"Maybe she had second thoughts," Conryu said.

"That's probably it. Let's go, Master."

"Let's not. I don't have anywhere to be, we can wait a while."

A while turned out to be fifteen minutes. Prime was flying back and forth in what served as demon book pacing, when the door swung open and in walked a tall, willowy woman in all white, her long blond hair swirling around her face in a breeze Conryu couldn't feel.

She looked at him with pure white eyes that sparked with

lightning. For a moment he could easily believe she was a real saint, fallen from Heaven.

Then her stern expression broke into a smile. "You must be Conryu Koda. I've heard so much about you, most of it good."

"Who said something bad?" Conryu had a pretty fair idea, but was curious to see if she'd tell him.

"Mrs. Alustrial, the first-year light magic teacher. She said you were too arrogant for your own good. I found her critique quite amusing given the source. She's had her nose out of joint ever since the midterm last year."

Conryu grinned. He and St. Seraphim were going to get along fine, he could feel it. That reminded him. "Is it Mrs. St. Seraphim?"

"No, just St. Seraphim. My mom named me that when she saw my eyes. She believed she gave birth to someone more than human. She hung herself the day after she brought me home from the hospital." St. Seraphim got a faraway look. "To this day I have no idea why."

Conryu stared for a moment. Why would she tell him something so personal five minutes after meeting him? "I'm sorry."

"It's okay. I never knew her so I didn't get very upset when I found out. So, what do you want to learn?"

The abrupt change of subject jarred him a bit. "Healing. Of all the skills I lack, that's the one I regret most."

"Oh, good. Most of my students want to learn to throw lightning or showy things like that. Healing is really the most important skill a light magic wizard can learn since it's what we're best at. There are plenty of other elements that are good for killing people."

Wasn't that the truth? "I healed my friend Kelsie using just willpower. The headache from the backlash wasn't nice."

She blinked her strange eyes. "You've already channeled light magic? How perfect. That should make it much easier for you to use it again. I think I'll just teach you the strongest healing spell I know. Only one in ten light magic wizards has the potential to cast it. It's called Touch of the Goddess."

They spent the next three hours practicing and when their time was up Conryu had successfully cast the spell twice. Prime never so much as fidgeted. It seemed light magic didn't bother him after all. Not that Conryu imagined that would stop Prime from complaining later.

* * *

After a day of gathering supplies and two days of nonstop hiking, an exhausted Yarik stood on a hill overlooking the wizard's academy. If he never had to walk through the woods again it would be too soon. At least the worst of the summer heat had passed, not that you'd know it from the sweat soaking his undershirt.

His discomfort was irrelevant; they'd made it and nothing else mattered. For some reason he'd expected something more out of the ordinary. While the two large buildings looked nice enough, certainly far nicer than most of the buildings in the Empire, nothing about the campus shouted "magic." Perhaps the builders intended it that way, he didn't know or care.

From his pack he pulled a pair of binoculars. A group of students stood on the lakeshore watching an older woman conjure a serpent of water. He shifted his line of sight to the ruins of a small bungalow sitting at the water's edge. Nothing much left, just a foundation and short dock stretching out over the water.

A frown formed and deepened as he continued to study the

campus. He'd never spot Anya from here. His only hope lay in watching the flow of students and hope he could figure out where she'd most likely go if something happened.

Yarik swapped his binoculars for a red crystal the size of a hen's egg. He peered through it and everything took on a red tint. A bright yellow line ran around the school. The witches had only given him the most rudimentary explanation of how the crystal worked, but one thing they stressed was that magical defenses would appear yellow. He had to assume the line served as some sort of early warning system.

"What do you see, Agent?" Hedon asked.

"Not much. We need to get closer, but there's some sort of protection in place."

"What sort of protection?" Victor asked.

"That's what we're going to find out." Yarik left his position at the edge of the hill and started around toward its base. The defensive line ran just ahead of it. He doubted it would be anything lethal. From what he'd observed, this country took great pains to safeguard its citizens' lives.

Twenty minutes later he checked the crystal again. The line ran just a few feet ahead of them.

Yarik raised his hand and eased forward, bracing himself in case he'd made a mistake about the softness of his enemies. His fingers broke the line and nothing happened, no zap, tingle, or change in the line when he viewed it through the crystal. Yarik shrugged and stepped all the way across.

Still nothing.

He turned and motioned Hedon to join him. The moment the dragon-blood broke the plane a jagged burst of energy shot toward the school.

"Hide!" Yarik said.

The three of them ran for a clump of boulders that had

fallen from a cliff face years ago. Five minutes later a woman in a pale-blue robe hovered in the sky above them. She looked all around, shrugged, and flew away.

Yarik let out a sigh. The ward reacted to magical beings, but not normal humans. That complicated things, but not too badly. A plan was quickly forming. For the first time since he arrived in the Alliance, Yarik saw a path to completing his mission.

5

ATTACK ON THE ACADEMY

For the next day and a half Yarik observed the school. He figured out which building was the dorm and which the lecture hall and had a rough idea of what time classes ended. When Sunday morning dawned his plan of attack was clear in his mind. Whether it would work or not time would tell, but if he failed he doubted he'd get another chance and he shuddered to think what might happen to his wife back home. No, he had to succeed. If he'd known how obsessed the czar truly was with Anya, he wouldn't have let her go in the first place.

When he lowered his binoculars for the last time Yarik found Hedon and Victor gnawing on beef jerky. The dragonbloods ate a remarkable amount of meat every day. Yarik's stomach was too twisty to even look at the remains of their food supply.

"Are you two ready?"

They finished the last of their breakfast and nodded.

78

"Okay. I'm going to sneak onto the grounds and activate the distraction. The moment I do you two need to break for the train platform. Seize the conductor and wait for me. We'll escape with Anya in the chaos. If you don't have control of the train when I arrive we're done. Questions?"

They'd been over the plan half a dozen times already and both warriors shook their heads. Yarik took a steadying breath and nodded. He was as ready as he could be. From their pack he removed a pocket knife, a revolver and a cylinder. That was all he took with him.

Yarik made his way through the forest toward the school. The supply train wasn't due to arrive until midmorning so he felt no need to rush. Instead he focused on the mission, getting his mind zeroed in on what he needed to do. The trickiest part would be finding Anya in a sea of girls. His chance lay in the hope that there weren't any girls of Imperial descent at the school. That might help her to stand out. It was a thin hope, but the only one he had.

Two hours later he reached the edge of the woods. From his position he couldn't see anyone moving around. Hopefully no one would spot him either.

Yarik popped open the cylinder and four mottled brown spheres rolled out onto the grass. He'd never seen the eggs before, but he'd read about the monsters that hatched from them. The process seemed simple enough. He took out his pocket knife and nicked his finger. A single drop of blood dripped down on each egg, soaking into the shell. The witch that gave him the eggs explained that this was the most important part of the process. His blood waking them would ensure that the creatures wouldn't attack him once they reached full size.

The first crack ran through one of the eggs. Soon the other three showed signs of life. A small dragon head surrounded by a scruff of dark fur emerged. The tiny talons of the baby dragon mane ripped the egg away revealing a scale-covered body the size of a gecko with withered wings on its back. Not the most awesome sight Yarik had ever seen.

Soon the creatures began moving around and growing. In seconds they were the size of house cats, then mastiffs. A minute after they hatched, the dragon manes had grown to the size of bulls and their wings spread over twice their height.

The four monsters each looked at him like a cat looks at a mouse. Yarik dearly hoped the witch hadn't led him astray with her instructions for waking them.

The dragon manes grew until they doubled in size again. The monsters continued to stare at Yarik through the transformation until he finally understood what they wanted.

He pointed toward the school. "Attack."

* * *

The first Sunday of the year meant Club Day. Conryu stood on the steps with Anya and Prime and looked out over the sea of tents. The alchemy club had roped Maria into helping drum up new members. They said since she was sort of famous after the attack this summer it might help them draw a crowd. She hadn't been thrilled with their reasons, but she agreed to help out anyway.

Kelsie had joined the cooking club the day they arrived at school, much to his surprise. When he asked why she said now that she wasn't rich she needed to learn to cook. That seemed as good a reason as any to join a club so he wished her luck.

Though he had joined the golem club last year, Conryu

didn't know if there was even going to be a golem club this year. He also wondered what they did with the Blinky mobile, but that was a whole other issue. Their leader and driving force graduated last year, leaving him and Crystal as the only members. Speaking of the tall earth wizard, he hadn't had time to talk to her yet what with watching over Anya every spare minute.

"So do you think you'll join a club?" Conryu asked. If she did, it might give him a little more free time.

"Only if it's one you're a member of." She adjusted her drab brown robe. It seemed almost a crime for the gorgeous freshman to have to wear the ugly, shapeless garment. "Still, there's no reason not to have a look around."

He agreed and they walked down the steps and over to the nearest tent. It was the crafts club. They made candles, incense, and other items useful in magical rituals. A spicy aroma drifted out of the tent. Whatever they were burning, it smelled nice.

Anya sighed. "I love cinnamon. It reminds me of a treat my mother used to make for me. Have you ever eaten baked apples?"

"No, but I've had apple pie."

"Same idea, but the apple bakes whole and without a crust. The inside gets soft and almost melts in your mouth."

"Sounds good." Conryu moved away from the crafts tent and toward the center aisle.

"I miss home sometimes. Mostly I miss feeling safe."

Conryu didn't know what to say to that. His parents were safe in the city and no one had tried to kill him in weeks. "You can relax a little here. There are a ton of powerful wizards around. Anybody thinking of attacking the academy would have to be insane."

A tremendous roar filled the air.

Did a spell run out of control? He looked around and found everyone else doing the same.

Anya trembled as she clung to him. "I know that sound. That's what the monsters that attacked the Ministry in London sounded like."

He sensed movement a moment before Prime said, "Master, above us!"

Conryu looked up to see a dragon covered in bronze scales circling overhead. Two more joined it while a fourth soared toward the dorm.

One of the girls noticed the dragons and screamed. Like a match to oil, fear exploded through the students. Girls ran in every direction. It was chaos and he didn't want to get caught up in it.

"I told you!" Anya screamed. "I told you they'd come for me."

"Yes, you did." Keeping his cool, Conryu focused on the earth at his feet and called to mind one of the defensive spells his earth magic teacher taught him. "Spirits of earth, strong and firm. A barrier form to prove your worth. Diamond Skin!"

Invisible energy rose through his feet and surrounded his body. The spell would protect him from all but the most powerful physical attacks.

"Let's find Maria and Kelsie and get inside."

One of the dragons dove and breathed fire, setting the poetry club's tent ablaze. Students came pouring out to join the mad dash.

Keeping Anya behind him, Conryu made his way toward the cooking club's tent. "Prime, keep an eye out for Kelsie and Maria."

A girl in red robes ran into Conryu, bounced off, and went

sprawling to the ground. Thanks to his spell he didn't even feel it.

"Are you okay?" She ignored him, scrambled to her feet, and raced toward the school. "I guess so."

A dragon dove toward a clump of fleeing students. When the fire roared to life in its mouth Conryu raised his hand. "Break!"

His spell doused the fire for a moment and the dragon pulled up, soaring back into the sky.

"Master, to your right."

He spotted Kelsie an instant later. She crouched just inside the tent entrance like it would offer her some protection.

Another roar from above drew his attention. Dean Blane and a handful of teachers were buzzing around the dragons, blasting them with spells. The attacks didn't seem to do much good, but at least the monsters were distracted for the time being.

Conryu pushed his way over to Kelsie. She clenched her eyes tight and her hands held the tent flap in an iron grip.

He knelt beside her. "Hey, are you hurt?"

Kelsie's eyes popped open and she lunged at him, wrapping her arms around his neck. Only his protective spell kept her from strangling him.

"What are those things?" The question came out as a half sob.

"Dragon manes," Anya said. "The Empire sent them, I'm sure of it."

Conryu didn't doubt it as they looked exactly like the monsters described in the report Mr. Kane let him read. Strange they didn't seem especially interested in Anya. Perhaps they were too stupid to pick her out amongst the throng.

"Have you seen Maria?" Conryu asked.

Kelsie gave a visible shake as she pulled herself together. "No, but the alchemy club set up four tents down."

"Let's go."

With Conryu once more in the lead they sprinted off. The crowd had thinned as more and more students fled the area. He spotted Maria waving people toward the school and the giant knot in his stomach untied. She was okay, thank goodness. Figured she'd keep her head too.

"Maria!" She turned his way and her look of relief brought a smile to his face. "We need to get out of here."

"No kidding."

Aside from a few stragglers the area around the tents was clear of students. The four of them joined the rush toward the front steps. Conryu held Maria's hand and Anya kept his arm in a death grip. Kelsie seemed to be managing okay on her own. Now that they were moving, her panic had subsided.

Conryu pushed through the doors and into the entry area. Hundreds of girls milled around, seeming uncertain what to do next. Conryu wasn't sure himself, but he doubted hanging around on the ground floor surrounded by glass was the best idea. They needed to get everyone downstairs. How was another matter altogether.

"What now?" Anya asked.

Conryu scanned the crowd. It didn't take long to spot Crystal. He whistled and when she looked his way motioned her over.

"You're a sight for sore eyes," Crystal said. "What the hell are those things?"

"Long story," Conryu said. "Can you get everyone downstairs? You're not safe here."

"I can try. They're all scared half to death. So am I for that matter. I saw the dean and some of the teachers fighting."

"Me too. I'm sure they'll have everything wrapped up in no time." Conryu hated lying, but he didn't want to frighten Crystal any more than she already was. "I'm afraid if one of them slams into the building everyone will get sprayed with glass."

"I hadn't even considered that." Crystal chewed her lip. "I'll see what I can do. What about you?"

"Those things might be after Anya. We're going up to the dean's office. That room's warded six ways from Sunday. We'll be okay."

Crystal nodded. "Good luck."

"You too."

Conryu led his companions through the press. Outside an especially loud roar sounded and the room shook. It felt like something big struck the ground nearby. He hoped that meant one of the monsters was down for the count.

They ran up to the administrative area. The secretaries had all made themselves scarce. At the end of the hall the door to the dean's office hung partway open.

Thank god for small favors. If Dean Blane had locked it he would have needed to break it down and that would sort of defeat the point of hiding there.

"Do you really think we'll be safe in her office?" Anya asked.

Conryu took a breath to say he had no idea when Maria cut in. "Of course we will. Dean Blane is crazy strong and her office will have plenty of protections in place."

He gave Maria's hand a squeeze of thanks. They took a step toward the open door.

The room shook and a dragon mane smashed through the wall, stopping between them and the office.

85

It lashed out with a wing and sent everyone flying.

Conryu tumbled and bounced, losing all sense of where the girls ended up.

At least his spell protected him. He leapt back to his feet. The dragon mane roared and opened its mouth. Flames danced behind its teeth.

Conryu raised his hand and focused all his anger. "Break!"

A head-sized ball of dark magic slammed into the monster's mouth, snuffed the flames, and staggered it.

Having bought a moment's respite, he scanned the area. Anya had landed behind him, farthest from the dragon mane. She was as safe as she could be under the current circumstances. Kelsie sat up in the middle of the hall, seeming no worse for the wear.

His heart skipped a beat. Maria leaned against the wall, head slumped and not moving.

Cold rage settled over him. "Shroud of all things ending. Cowl of nightmares born. Dark wrap that looks upon all things' doom, Reaper's Cloak!"

The chill of the cloak settled over him and he pulled the cowl up over his head. Maria's life force still burned in her chest. Thank goodness.

He turned his attention to the recovering dragon mane. A bright blue flame burned in its breast, but not for long.

* * *

Yarik gave the dragon manes a short headstart then followed. As he topped the hill, he found a scene of chaos. Girls in robes ran every which way, tents burned, and everyone was screaming. The dragons flew above the gathering. Every once in a while one of them dove and breathed fire, setting another tent ablaze.

A dragon mane peeled off and slammed into the dorm. From the number of people milling around he doubted any of the students were inside – at least he hoped so. While Yarik needed to capture Anya to save his wife, he'd prefer to avoid any innocent people getting hurt.

A black sphere shot up at a descending dragon and snuffed out its flame. Yarik tracked it back to its source and found a short-haired figure in black robes standing beside a blond in brown. He was too far away to be sure, but his gut said the blond was Anya. Over his years in the security service he'd learned to trust that feeling.

Yarik followed the pair as they ran deeper into the chaos. They collected a girl in black then another in white. The little group was among the last to head for the school building. Yarik jogged along behind them. He silently cursed himself for not thinking to grab something he could use to simulate a robe. He shook his head and kept going. Hopefully the girls would be too upset to take any notice of him.

He coughed as a cloud of smoke came his way. Ducking his head, Yarik pushed through the doors in time to see the students he'd been following run up a set of stairs. He circled the largest gathering of students and eased up behind them.

He found a door swinging and peeked through the small window. The building shook as a dragon mane smashed its way into the building. Its wing slammed into the group, scattering them like tenpins.

If the stupid beast killed Anya, he'd...well he probably wouldn't do anything, but the czar would certainly have Yarik and his wife executed. He let out the breath he'd been holding when she climbed to her feet.

The boy in black faced the dragon mane. In fact, everyone was looking at the giant dragon. He doubted he'd get a better chance than this. Yarik pulled his revolver, eased the door open, and came up behind Anya.

He clamped his hand over her mouth and pressed the muzzle of his gun to her back. "Make a sound and you're dead," he whispered.

She stiffened, but remained silent. The boy was chanting in one of the wizard's unintelligible languages, totally focused on the dragon mane. The beast had done its job well.

Yarik dragged Anya back out the door. When it shut he pushed her toward the steps. "Move."

She looked back at him and her eyes widened. "You! Why are you here? You let me go in Calais."

"A mistake. A moment of weakness. One I'm here to fix. Now move."

She looked more sad than afraid. Yarik hated her for the pity he saw in her eyes.

He poked her with the muzzle of his gun. They trotted down the steps to the now-empty lobby. Outside wizards fought two of the dragon manes in the sky above the school.

They ran through the burning tents toward the train platform. Hopefully Hedon and Victor had the conductor under control so they could leave at once. Any delay might prove fatal.

* * *

"At last you choose to embrace my power," the cold voice of the Reaper said.

Conryu hated that voice, but right now he had a monster to

deal with and minimal options. Maria was hurt and he needed to end this quickly.

"Yes, damn you. How do I kill that thing?"

"All creatures of draconic lineage have some resistance to magic, but nothing can resist death. I am Null, the Reaper, Ender of all Things. Call my name and imagine the beast's life being snuffed out and it will be."

Such a simple thing. Out of the corner of his eye he saw Maria lying, unmoving, on the floor. The dragon mane roared and stared at her.

Conryu's eyes narrowed. It wouldn't hurt her again, he refused to allow it.

He raised his hand and focused on the blue flame burning in the dragon mane's chest, imagining it vanishing. "Null take you!"

A ghostly, skeletal hand stretched out from him and wrapped around the dragon mane's soul. The creature's deep roar turned to a pained squeal as the ghost hand closed.

It thrashed and smashed several desks before going still, its life force annihilated. The monster's scales turned gray and the light went out of its eyes.

"See, boy, nothing to it. Why not go help your teachers? We can slay the remaining beasts in seconds. Then we can hunt down the Le Fay Society. You know they'll be after you sooner or later."

The Reaper had a point. It would be simple enough to kill anyone that might threaten him or the people he cared about. Might even make the world a better place. He had this power whether he wanted it or not. Why not use it?

"Conryu!"

Kelsie's shout dragged him out of his morbid musings.

89

Cursing the Reaper and his evil power, he willed the spell to end.

Never again.

There was a moment's delay and the Reaper said, "Never say never, boy. You will need me again."

Voice and cloak vanished together and light returned to the world. Kelsie knelt beside Maria. Her hands shook and waved around.

"What happened to her?" Conryu joined them on the floor.

"She hit her head." Kelsie looked at him with tears in her eyes. "I don't know how to help."

"I do." He'd only had two lessons with St. Seraphim, but the first spell he memorized was one of powerful healing. "The gentle light of Heaven washes away all wounds, Touch of the Goddess."

Conryu's hand glowed with golden light and he brushed it across Maria's forehead. He willed the energy along with his love to sink into her and heal whatever injury she suffered.

The glow expanded and enveloped Maria's whole body. When it faded she groaned and sat up. "What happened?"

Conryu grinned. "You got walloped by a dragon, but I think you'll be okay."

"I know I will, thanks to you. What spell did you use?" Typical Maria, more interested in the spell than the actual healing.

"Touch of the Goddess. Are you familiar with it?"

She stared at him for a moment. "I've read about it, but it's a master-level spell usable only by the most powerful light-magic-aligned wizards. How do you know it?"

"St. Seraphim taught it to me Wednesday. Considering the trouble we always get into I figured knowing a healing spell would come in handy." He reached down and brushed a stray hair off her forehead. "It certainly did today."

"Where's Anya?" Kelsie asked.

"Shit! She was right behind me." Conryu gave Maria one last squeeze on the shoulder and got to his feet.

Last time her saw her Anya had been standing by the door to the stairwell. Conryu shoved the door open and looked over the rail. No sign of her.

She wouldn't have gone off on her own, Anya was far too jittery for that. He ran across the hall and over to the hole. The dead dragon already stank like it had been rotting for a month.

He squinted against the glare. A dragon mane swooped past him with a pair of wizards in pursuit.

When his field of vision cleared, he spotted two figures running across the yard. He muttered the water spell Terra taught him and they seemed to leap towards him. One was a blond in a brown robe, definitely Anya. The second was a man in a sweat-stained suit. He had a pistol in his hand, which explained how he got Anya to go with him, but who was he and how did he get here?

It didn't matter. Conryu needed to stop him and save Anya.

He snorted. Some bodyguard. He'd been at it barely a week and his charge already got kidnapped.

He turned back to Maria and Kelsie. If another dragon mane attacked, there was no way the two of them could defeat it. Did he go after Anya or stay and protect Maria and Kelsie?

Conryu wanted to shout. He needed to be in two places at once.

"What's going on?" Maria asked. Kelsie had helped her sit up.

"Someone grabbed Anya."

"What are you standing here for? Go help her."

"What about you two? You're not in any shape for a fight."

"We'll be fine," Maria said. "Get going."

He nodded. "Okay. Be careful. I'll be back as soon as I can."

Conryu returned to the hole and glanced over his shoulder. The girls were blocked by a wall, good. Before casting his flight spell he whispered, "Kai."

The girl in black faded into view and took a knee. "Chosen. I saw everything, sensed his presence. You were in direct communion with the Reaper. I feel like a fool for ever doubting you."

He looked back again, but the girls hadn't reacted to her low voice. "Thanks. I need you to watch over Maria and Kelsie. I'm trusting you with their safety. Don't let me regret it."

She met his gaze, her eyes hard and determined. "My life for theirs, Chosen."

When Kai had disappeared again Conryu released his diamond skin and cast, "Father of winds, carry me into your domain. Air Rider."

Power swirled around him and he leapt out of the hole. Like a missile, Conryu streaked toward the fleeing kidnapper.

* * *

By the time Conryu got up into the air he'd lost sight of Anya. He didn't dare fly too fast for fear of missing something, so he glided along, scanning the ground as he flew in the direction he'd last seen them running. He hadn't been more than a minute or two getting after them so they couldn't have gotten far.

"See anything, Prime?"

"No, Master. Are you well? I felt the Reaper's presence again back there."

"I'm fine. I didn't want to use his power, but I was pressed for time."

"Null's power is certainly the most efficient way to kill something."

He grimaced. Conryu had no desire for a more efficient way to kill.

Half a minute later he spotted Anya and the stranger running toward the train platform. A second man was waiting, a big, bald bruiser that had to be seven feet tall. However big he was, Conryu doubted he'd last long against a wizard.

With a thought he descended toward the platform. Anya spotted him and shouted, "Conryu!"

So much for the element of surprise. The moment he touched the ground Conryu chanted, "Spirits of earth, strong and firm. A barrier form to prove your worth. Diamond Skin!"

Power rose up and surrounded him and not a moment too soon as a bullet from the kidnapper's revolver bounced off his thigh.

Conryu raised his hand to disintegrate the gun, but the big man stepped into his path.

"Go, Agent," the giant said. "I will deal with the wizard."

"Good luck, Victor." The kidnapper shoved Anya onto the train ahead of him and followed her.

"I don't want to hurt you," Conryu said. "Just move aside so I can go help my friend."

"I can't do that." A faint glow surrounded Victor and scales appeared on his arms and neck. His eyes glowed yellow. "I offer you the chance to withdraw. You are not my target."

Conryu grimaced. What sort of creature did he face? He guessed this was one of the dragon-blood warriors mentioned in the report Mr. Kane showed him. Conryu never fought one before, but it couldn't be stronger than a demon, right?

He thrust a hand out. "All things burn to ash, Inferno Blast!"

Searing flames washed over Victor. Conryu snapped his fist shut. He'd expected the dragon-blood to dive out of the way so he could chase after Anya.

When the flames vanished Victor stood unharmed. His shirt was burned away, revealing a scale-covered chest.

"Careful, Master. Dragon-bloods are resistant to magic."

"Thank you, oh master of the obvious."

Victor drew a breath and exhaled a pale-blue cloud.

"Break!" Conryu's dark magic negated the attack.

"Our magic seems evenly matched," Victor said.

The dragon-blood roared and charged, scale-covered fists raised. Conryu sidestepped and deflected a right cross. Only his protective spell kept the heavy blow from breaking his arm. The dragon-blood punched harder than the zombie thing he fought in the sewer last summer.

The left came next. Conryu stepped in and countered with a straight-fingered thrust to his opponent's elbow joint.

The scales were so strong his fingers didn't penetrate.

Victor tried to bite him. Conryu ducked to avoid it.

A back flip to create space.

Out of the corner of his eye he noticed the train moving.

That distraction proved costly as Victor stepped in and caught him on the cheek with a right cross.

Conryu went flying, bounced, and popped to his feet. Bright spots swam in his vision. Even Diamond Skin didn't fully absorb the blow.

You know how to stop him, a chill voice whispered in the back of his mind.

He ignored the Reaper and ducked another powerful blow. He needed space to cast.

Conryu slipped a straight right, danced behind Victor, and kicked him with everything he had in the back of the knee.

The joint gave and Conryu sprinted twenty yards clear of his opponent.

Diamond Skin wasn't the only earth spell his teacher had shown him. "Fists of stone, bind and hold, Stone Grasp!"

Conryu slammed his palm on the ground and pictured two massive hands rising out of the cement and grasping his opponent's ankles.

The earth spirits obliged and as Victor climbed to his feet stone hands grabbed him, locking him in place.

"Clever, Master. His magic resistance only weakens spells targeting him directly."

Conryu ignored Prime and focused on his spell. Two more hands shot out of the ground, wrapping around Victor's wrists and leaving the dragon-blood thoroughly trapped.

"We have to catch up to Anya. Father of winds, carry me into your domain. Air Rider." The spell lifted Conryu a foot off the ground, spun him around and flipped him upside down.

"Your mind is too muddled to concentrate, Master. You need to rest."

Conryu tried to focus, but the dancing lights and pain in his cheek were too much. He got turned right side up and ended the spell.

"She's getting further away every moment, Prime. I was supposed to protect her."

"So you will." Prime flew down so their eyes were level. "Do you imagine it will be difficult for a school full of wizards to track Anya down?"

"No, I expect not. I just don't like to lose."

"How do you think he feels?" Prime asked.

They turned as one to look at the bound and snarling

dragon-blood. Didn't look like he enjoyed losing either. Too bad.

Struggle as he might, Victor didn't have strength enough to break free of the stone. Should be safe to leave him there for now. Maybe Dean Blane could drag something out of the creature.

Conryu turned toward the school and began the long trudge back. The grounds were silent, so he assumed the teachers had dealt with the remaining dragon manes. That meant Maria and Kelsie were safe. Thank goodness for small favors.

At the top of the little hill that led to the campus Conryu stopped and stared at the ruins of Club Day. Two giant corpses littered the grass between smoldering tents. Deep furrows marred the ground. The combined stench of char and torn flesh filled the air. It resembled some movie director's vision of Hell.

Giving a tired shake of his head, Conryu started down. However big the mess, it wouldn't take a few hundred wizards long to set it all right. The hardest part would be dealing with the corpses. Where did you bury something that big? Maybe they could just disintegrate them.

He pushed through the doors and found the lobby still empty. No one had called the other students up from the basement. Everything seemed calm enough now, but that wasn't his decision to make.

Up in the administrative area he found Maria on her feet, which took a weight off his chest. Dean Blane stood staring at the dragon mane corpse with her hands on her hips.

She spun, spotted him, and frowned. "Did you leave this rotting corpse in front of my office?"

Conryu stared at her for a moment then laughed. He kept

laughing as Maria hugged him and Kelsie hugged him and even Dean Blane hugged him.

When he got himself under control, he wiped his eyes and said, "An Imperial agent escaped with Anya. He had a dragon-blood with him. I captured the monster, but he held me off long enough for his master to escape on the train. They fled toward the city."

"Is she okay?" Maria asked.

"For the moment." Conryu sighed. "I'm pretty sure they want her alive, so I doubt they'll do anything to her."

"I'll alert Central." Dean Blane looked over the ruined desks then inched around the dead monster and went into her office.

Conryu hoped they sent a large force to meet the train. If there were more dragon-bloods, whoever showed up would have their hands full.

* * *

When Conryu came flying out of the sky Anya imagined herself saved, but the dragon-blood warrior moved to intercept him and the agent dragged her into the train. Now they were rushing away from the school at a terrifying speed. She'd never been in a vehicle like this back home. The train moved so smoothly it was like they were motionless. Only the trees whizzing by out the window revealed the truth. Even though it was her second trip the magic of it astounded her.

The agent dragged her to the front of the train where a second giant man stood beside a trembling woman who held her hands on a complex control panel. She wore a gray uniform and a faint glow surrounded her hands. A wizard then, which made sense if the train ran on magic.

"How long to reach the city?" the agent asked.

"At this speed, fifteen minutes." Despite her shaking the wizard's voice held firm.

"Good. Do as you're told and you'll live through this."

"Where's Victor?" the giant man asked.

"He stayed behind to hold off the wizard that came to her rescue. I fear he's either dead or captured by now. I'm sorry, Hedon. It was an unfortunate, but necessary, sacrifice."

"No matter, Agent. To complete the czar's mission, no sacrifice is too great."

"Keep an eye on things up here," the agent said. "I have to find something to tie her up with."

"I could just break both her arms," Hedon offered.

Anya's head spun. How had it come to this?

"I'm not sure the czar would appreciate us delivering his new White Witch in less than ideal condition."

"As you think best, Agent."

The agent dragged Anya out of the control room and back into a cargo area filled with bins and crates of food, mostly fruits and vegetables.

"Why are you doing this?" Anya asked. "If you intended to bring me to the czar, why let me go in the first place? You seem like a decent person, or so I thought. What's your name?"

"Yarik." He blew out a sigh. "I had no wish to come here and bring you back. I believed, foolishly it turns out, that the czar might accept your escape, especially once you reached the Kingdom of the Isles. I have a wife, you see, and the czar made it very clear that if you escaped again it wouldn't just be my neck in the noose."

Anya stared. "I'm so sorry. I had no idea."

"Don't pity me. My own mistakes brought me here." He rummaged through the bins and came up with a bungee cord.

"I've served in the security services for over twenty years. It didn't take a genius to see how the Empire used people, ground them up and spit them out. I accepted it, hell, I worked to stop those trying to make a difference even knowing how screwed up the system was. I did it because they didn't have a chance. They still don't."

"So what changed?" Anya asked.

He barked a humorless laugh. "I got to know a witch. Just a kid, maybe two or three years older than you. She put on a brave face, but underneath she was scared more than anything."

"What was her name?" Anya held out her hands for Yarik to tie.

"Irmina. She was killed by the rebels helping you escape. That's what I tried to tell myself, but the truth is the Empire killed her. I wanted to spare you that fate. I still want to spare you, but I can't save you and my wife." He shrugged.

"You could turn yourself in and ask for the Alliance's help. I've met some good people here. It's not like back home."

"Perhaps not, but I promise you no one in this government will risk a conflict with the Empire to save one person. The only way to protect her is to bring you back. I hate it, but that's the way it is."

The train slowed and Yarik dragged her back to the control room. Ahead of them waited the largest building Anya had ever seen. Standing in front of it was a group of men in armor carrying machine guns. They'd gathered behind a pair of black vehicles with golden scales painted on them.

"A welcoming committee," Yarik said. "Terrific."

"She must have warned them." Hedon squeezed the conductor's neck and Anya heard the spine snap. Her stomach twisted and she swallowed hard. "I will deal with them."

"Leave one of the vehicles intact," Yarik said. "They look a lot better than our piece-of-shit pickup."

"We escape in their own car." Hedon flashed a toothy smile. "I like that."

The dragon-blood brushed past her, his scales appearing as he went. Anya shuddered. Those poor people didn't stand a chance.

6

SUCCESS AND FAILURE

onryu flew along above the highway, a small tracking device in his hand. Below him hundreds of cars zoomed along on their way to and from Central. Dean Blane's warning had arrived in time, but the team sent in to capture the Imperials was woefully inadequate to deal with a dragon-blood warrior. Fourteen elite soldiers died in the attempt, all of them torn to pieces. Conryu didn't see the pictures and he didn't want to; he could imagine them well enough, having felt the monster's strength himself.

What he didn't understand was why they'd steal one of the Department's cars. Did they not know about tracking software? Maybe it wasn't something available in their empire. Either way, it worked out for Conryu. The dean provided him a portable tracking unit and programed it to locate the stolen car.

He didn't ask for any backup and frankly doubted any of the teachers would have been able to join him anyway given the state of the school. Instead, everyone warned him to be careful, especially Maria since she'd insisted on healing his minor concussion herself. They didn't need to worry. No way would he underestimate the dragon-blood a second time.

The tracker beeped, focusing him on the matter at hand. According to the tiny screen the stolen car was a little ways ahead of him. He flew lower and scanned the lanes.

Bingo! A black SUV in the center lane. That was his target. Now, how to get it to pull over without hurting Anya?

"Perhaps you could target a tire," Prime said.

"Blowing out a tire might cause them to lose control and flip over. If she isn't buckled in it might kill Anya. No, I think I'll take out the engine."

He flew above them for a while, watching for a rest area. Hopefully the kidnappers would be smart enough to pull off rather than try to fight in the middle of a three-lane highway.

Five miles up the road he spotted it, a nice, quiet little rest area. A pair of cars were already there, but no big crowds. That suited him perfectly.

Conryu focused his will on the hood of the stolen car and pictured the engine disintegrating. "Shatter!"

Dark magic crashed into the metal and reduced it to rust. The stolen car slowed at once and the driver pulled off, exactly as Conryu had hoped he would. The SUV rolled to a stop and Conryu landed in front of it, renewing his defensive spell.

A big, bald man sat in the passenger seat so the man behind the steering wheel had to be the kidnapper. They stared at him and he stared back. After half a minute of waiting Conryu crooked his finger, beckoning them out.

The dragon-blood obliged him. This one could have been a brother to the one he captured back at the train platform. Having learned from his earlier encounter, Conryu didn't waste time with any of his weaker spells.

"Fists of stone, bind and hold, Stone Grasp!" He slapped the ground and willed the magic to activate.

Stone hands formed in an instant. The dragon-blood leapt clear before they could grasp his ankles.

Conryu grinned and kept pouring magic into the ground. The stone hands shot up and snatched his opponent out of the air and yanked him to the dirt. Arms of rock wrapped around the dragon-blood, binding him in place.

"That's quite enough." The kidnaper had Anya in front of him and the barrel of his pistol at her temple. A black bungee cord bound her hands in front of her. She looked scared, but unharmed. "Back away or she dies."

Conryu focused on the weapon. *Shatter!*

The gun exploded in a burst of metal filings. Anya elbowed the man in the gut, breaking his grip. She ran to Conryu and ducked behind him.

"I think we're done here," Conryu said. "Surrender and I promise I won't hurt you."

The kidnapper slumped and hung his head. "You may as well kill me."

Conryu looked at Anya. "You okay?"

She nodded and held out her hands. A burst of dark magic removed the bindings. Anya took a step around him and towards the kidnapper.

Conryu jumped in front of her. "Whoa, what are you doing?"

"It's okay. Yarik didn't really want to capture me. In fact, he let me escape back in France. The only reason he came after me now is because his wife is still back in the Empire. If he fails, she dies."

"Traitor!" The dragon-blood roared and thrashed against the stone arms holding him down.

Yarik looked up. "I suppose I am a traitor. But what I mostly am is tired. Tired of running down enemies the Empire created themselves, tired of always being afraid, and more than anything, tired of seeing innocent people suffer for the czar's arrogance. Perhaps if you kill me, kill us both, the czar will spare Iliana."

Conryu had no intention of killing anyone now that Anya was safe. He also didn't intend to let an innocent woman die. "Would you be willing to defect and tell the government everything you know if your wife wasn't in danger?"

"Conryu?" Anya said.

He ignored her and focused on Yarik. The Imperial agent met his gaze. "The Empire is rotten. I've seen it myself far too many times to count. If Iliana is safe, I will help you tear it down any way I can."

"I'm not sure this is a good idea, Master."

"Of course it's a good idea. Saving an innocent life is always a good idea. Kai."

The ninja faded into view. "Yes, Chosen."

Anya grabbed his arm in a death grip. He patted her hand. "Relax, Kai's on my team. Stay with Anya and keep an eye on the prisoner. When they saw the car stop the Department should have dispatched reinforcements. As soon as you see them approaching vanish. I'm not ready to explain you to anyone."

Kai bowed. "As you wish."

Conryu eased his arm out of Anya's grip. "This won't take long. I may even return before the cavalry arrives. Kai will keep you safe. You can trust her."

"Be careful." Anya gave him a quick kiss on the cheek. "And thanks for coming after me."

"If I were any kind of bodyguard, you wouldn't have gotten

WRATH OF THE DRAGON CZAR

captured in the first place." He gave Anya's hand one last squeeze and turned to Yarik. "Ready?"

"For what?"

"To go get your wife."

* * *

Roman sat on his throne and stared as General Ivan related the details of his miserable defeat. His entire detachment killed, the fort lost, and him the only survivor. He tried to make it sound heroic, a courageous stand against impossible odds, but the fear stink rolling off him told Roman all he needed to know. Talon spared Ivan and returned him as a messenger boy. It wasn't an act of kindness either. The vampire had to know what Roman would do to the useless fool.

Only a handful of advisors stood beside the throne today. No need for the entire court to hear the details of Ivan's failure. A subordinate's failure made him look weak and that was one thing Roman couldn't allow. If he looked vulnerable it gave people ideas, the sort of ideas that made his life complicated. Roman hated complications. Though he now ruled one of the largest empires ever, at heart he remained a simple soldier. When presented with a problem his instinct was to attack.

General Ivan was his current problem.

When the general fell silent Roman asked, "So how did the vampires get into the fort to disable the wards?"

"They sent an ordinary human. He snuck in and used some sort of item to destroy them."

"A single man snuck past the many guards you placed on

the pillar? The one thing Nosorova warned you absolutely had to be protected at all costs."

"I set only a single guard." Ivan flinched as though expecting Roman to strike. And well he might. "How could I know the vampires had human servants capable of such a feat?"

"You should have assumed it!" Roman roared and surged to his feet. "You should have posted enough guards that a squad of humans wouldn't have been able to reach the pillar."

"Majesty I—"

Roman's clawed hand wrapping around his throat strangled off Ivan's excuse. It took no effort for him to lift the useless human off the ground.

"You've failed me, General." Roman gathered power in his chest. "I don't intend to give you the chance to do so again."

Roman exhaled an icy mist that enveloped Ivan. When it cleared the general had been frozen solid. Roman slammed his frozen body to the floor sending pieces of icy flesh flying everywhere.

If he wanted this vampire matter solved, he'd have to do it himself. But how? For all his personal power and the might of his army, at night they were no match for the undead. He needed an edge. Something that would allow him to hold the monsters at bay during the night.

"Damned vampires!" Roman roared at the ceiling setting one of the golden chandeliers trembling.

"Majesty."

Roman spun to see who dared to speak. The masked witch, Lady Wolf, had stepped forward. The woman had courage, he'd grant her that. He'd also grant her a swift death if he didn't like what she said.

"Speak."

"I've been considering your vampire problem and I believe I have a solution. The Society has in its possession an artifact left behind by the elves. The device is called the Solar Orb. If you feed light magic energy into it, the orb will produce an energy field that mimics sunlight."

"It will kill the undead?" If the artifact did what she said it would indeed solve his problem. With that artifact protecting his army, he could slaughter the vampires wherever they hid.

"Alas, no."

He tensed, ready to rip her head off, mask and all, for wasting his time.

"It isn't true sunlight, however, it will induce the paralysis that strikes them when the sun is out. It would be a simple matter for a strong man with a silver sword to take the head of an immobile enemy."

Roman relaxed. It wasn't a perfect solution, but the woman had a point. A helpless vampire was an easy kill even for his weakest soldier.

"And you'd be willing to provide this artifact?"

"It is one of the more valuable items in our collection. That said, I believe an exchange might be possible. You have some elf artifacts, correct?"

Roman saw it clearly now. Good relations she claimed. Ha! The Society wanted something from his collection, it was as simple as that. She'd been building up to this moment since he first laid eyes on her. The discovery made him feel oddly better. Now that he understood her motivation, Roman trusted the woman more.

"I assume you had something in mind?"

"In point of fact I did."

"I'll bet." Roman dismissed his advisors with a wave. "Let's take a walk and see what we can come up with."

* * *

A giddy Lady Wolf left the czar's trophy room and nearly leapt for joy. He'd agreed to trade her the artifact fragment without even batting an eye. In fact, the czar had seemed surprised by her choice. For all his power the fool clearly had no idea what most of his collection did. They were status symbols to him, pretty trinkets he could look at and think how powerful he was. Such a waste. She'd noticed several items in her brief moment of study that would increase her personal power by an order of magnitude.

She sighed and headed for her chamber. This was neither the time nor place to be considering herself, not when they'd finally made a good step toward freeing Morgana. If Lady Tiger was right about the other half of the artifact, they might be able to claim it and complete their mission this year. And then the world would tremble before the might of their mistress.

Smiling behind her mask, Lady Wolf slipped into her room and activated her wards. Lady Dragon would be so pleased. She went straight to the mirror and activated the communication spell. The wait seemed interminable, but it probably lasted only a minute or two.

When Lady Dragon appeared she said, "You have news?"

"Indeed. I've arranged a trade for the item we seek. He'll give it to us in exchange for the Solar Orb."

"A steep price, but well worth it. Excellent job, Lady Wolf. When will you be making the trade?"

"The czar is eager to begin his war against the vampires. He will trade as soon as you can send the orb to me."

"Shall we meet in the realm of wind in an hour?" Lady Dragon asked.

"That would be perfect. I'll be there."

The mirror went blank. Lady Wolf needed to get out of the palace so she could open a portal. She wasn't under house arrest or anything, but the witches kept an eye on her. She felt them watching every moment she was out of her suite.

Well, if anyone asked she'd tell them the truth. She was running an errand for their precious master.

Outside, the hall was empty and as she made her way to the nearest exit she encountered no witches or others beyond a young serving girl overloaded with clean towels. Perhaps the czar had explained the situation to his people, so they were staying out of her way.

She didn't know and didn't care. Once she made the exchange, she'd leave this wretched land and return to civilization. When she reached one of the less used doors, she pushed it opened and stepped outside.

The gray, threatening sky did nothing to diminish her mood. She called the wind portal spell to mind. As a water-aligned wizard it didn't come naturally to her, but water and wind got along well enough that she shouldn't encounter any dangers.

Lady Wolf would have preferred to meet in the realm of water, where her powers were strongest, but Lady Dragon was fire aligned and not at all welcome in the realm of water. Besides, though they were allies, the members of the Society always used a neutral element if they had to meet outside the human realm. Not that anyone expected a betrayal, but given their naturally ambitious nature why risk it?

A gust of wind sent her hair swirling around her as she stepped through the portal. The realm of wind held a few crystal islands, but by and large remained empty of solid surfaces. All the spirits here knew how to fly after all. Lady

Wolf relaxed and opened her mind. When Lady Dragon entered the realm she'd sense it at once and they could meet halfway.

Aside from a few curious pixies, nothing bothered her. When she sensed Lady Dragon she willed herself in that direction. In the spirit realms time had little meaning and before she knew it Lady Wolf floated in front of her superior.

Lady Dragon held a clear crystal orb the size of her fist. Multifaceted and gleaming, the Solar Orb seemed to glow with its own inner light.

"Congratulations, Lady Wolf. I never would have imagined you completing your mission this quickly."

Lady Wolf bowed her head, humbly accepting the rare compliment. More because that's what Lady Dragon expected than because she felt especially humble. "Circumstances fell in my favor. I hope to make the exchange and return to headquarters by the end of the day."

"Good, we have a great deal of work to do in preparation for freeing Morgana."

"How goes Lady Tiger's search for the other half of the artifact?"

"She's found it, but hasn't provided me with any more details. That may change in the near future, time will tell." Lady Dragon held out the orb.

"I'll take that, thank you."

A woman in white emerged from the winds. How did one of the witches follow her without her noticing?

A second and third witch joined her, surrounding Lady Wolf and Lady Dragon. It seemed the czar preferred to take what he wanted by force.

The Scepter of Morgana appeared in Lady Dragon's hand

while the orb vanished. "You dare challenge the Supreme Hierarch of the Le Fay Society?"

Lady Wolf hesitated. If the czar wanted to take the orb by force, he would have waited until she arrived to trade, then overwhelmed her. Sending three witches out here made no sense.

"The czar didn't send you, did he?" Lady Wolf asked.

"Why should His Majesty have to trade with the likes of you when we can simply take the artifact?" the lead witch said, not really answering her question.

"Enough conversation." Lady Dragon thrust the scepter at the nearest witch and spoke a single harsh syllable in the language of fire. A crimson lance shot out and pierced the woman through the chest. She burst into flames and her ashes were scattered by the screaming winds.

The enemy leader chanted and hurled blades of compressed wind.

Lady Wolf countered in Infernal. "Break!"

The dark magic sphere scattered the attack, rendering it harmless.

A second witch screamed as blue-white flames engulfed her. Lady Dragon certainly wasn't taking it easy on their opponents. As expected from the Supreme Hierarch of the Society. She never took it easy on anyone.

When only the leader remained Lady Dragon gestured with her scepter, trapping the woman in a cage of flame. The witch attempted to cut through the cage with a gust of wind, but Lady Dragon twisted the spell and used the energy to make the flames burn hotter.

They flew up to face the trapped witch. She wasn't much more than a girl.

"Anastasia sent you, did she not?" Lady Wolf asked.

"No one sent us," the sweat-plastered girl said. "We heard you talking to the czar and thought to earn his favor by seizing the artifact ourselves."

"Who is Anastasia?" Lady Dragon asked.

"The White Witches' leader. I don't think she appreciates that I've gained the czar's good will. She may not have sent these fools directly, but I sense her hand in it."

"Does this affect our deal?"

"No, the czar wants the orb. I doubt he has any idea what these three did nor will he care."

"Good." Lady Dragon snapped her fingers and the cage contracted, cutting the girl into square chunks. "You'd best get back."

Lady Dragon put her scepter away and recalled the orb. She handed it over, nodded and flew back the way she'd come.

Lady Wolf hefted the orb. It weighed more than she'd expected for something so small. That was the thing about elf artifacts, they seldom ended up being what you expected.

* * *

Conryu and Yarik moved a little ways away from the girls. He placed a finger on Yarik's chest and cast, "Cloak of Darkness." The spell covered him in a protective shell of dark magic so he wouldn't suffer too much harm from his trip through Hell.

Yarik looked down at himself. "What have you done to me?"

"It's a simple protective spell. Where we're going, it isn't safe to travel without taking precautions. Plus, if you think about betraying me I can snuff your life out in an instant."

"I have no intention of betraying you now. What would I gain?"

"Not a thing." Conryu offered his best evil smile. "Now, let's get going. Reveal the way through infinite darkness. Open the path. Hell Portal!"

The black portal disk appeared and Yarik took a step back. Conryu waved to Anya and Kai, grabbed Yarik by the collar, and shoved him through. They'd barely entered the endless darkness of Hell when Cerberus came bounding up, one head growling and eyeing Yarik.

The security agent scrambled to get away, but Conryu held on tight. "Relax, Cerberus is going to guide us to your wife. I need you to focus on her. Picture Iliana and your home, every detail you can. Hold the image firmly in your mind. Can you do that?"

Yarik closed his eyes and sighed. "I see it every time I stop to think."

Conryu laid a hand on Cerberus's chest and focused on extending his link with the demon dog to Yarik. He didn't actually know if what he wanted to do was possible, but by now he'd come to realize that if you wanted something bad enough, the magic would often find a way to make it happen, though you might end up paying a price.

"Do you see her, boy? We need to find that lady. She's in trouble and we're going to help her. Can you find her for me?"

Cerberus panted and looked left and right. After half a minute the demon dog gave out a triple bark.

"Good boy." Conryu willed himself up onto Cerberus's back and dragged Yarik along with him. The Imperial agent shook from head to toe. Conryu didn't know if it was from fear or if it was an effect of being in Hell. Either way they needed to hurry. "He's got the scent now. Hold on tight. Let's hunt!"

Cerberus leapt forward and Conryu had the feeling of racing along though there was no real way to measure their progress in the void of Hell.

As they ran Prime said, "That was impressive, Master. When did you learn to share your link to Cerberus?"

"I didn't, it was instinctive, like most of the crazy shit I try. I'm just glad it worked."

Sometime later Cerberus stopped and let out a bark.

"What's going on?" Yarik asked. The Imperial agent had remained silent for the entire trip.

"Cerberus says we're here." Conryu hopped down and Yarik joined him. "Let's take a look. Grant me the power to see through realms, Vision Gate!"

A window into the mortal realm shimmered into existence revealing a small cabin on a grassy lot. A pair of white-uniformed soldiers armed with machine guns stood outside on either side of the door.

"Is that it?" Conryu asked.

Yarik stared, a look of pained longing twisting his face. "Yes. I've wanted so badly to return. It seems like another life when we lived here in peace. The job used to just be a job, you know. For a while I even thought I was doing good, protecting the people."

Yarik reached out, but his hand passed through the image like smoke. The portal shifted at Conryu's mental command, swinging around to the rear of the house. No more guards on the outside.

They moved through the wall, revealing a simple three-room interior. A tired-looking woman with dark hair and circles under her eyes sat knitting in a rocking chair.

"Iliana." Yarik breathed the words so softly Conryu barely heard them.

It looked like the guys outside were the only guards. He could deal with them no problem. The image pulled back and settled into place ten feet from the guards. Conryu transformed the viewing window into an actual Hell portal.

He raised a hand and stepped through, focusing on the guards' weapons. "Shatter!"

Both guns disintegrated in an instant. Conryu charged and before the stunned soldiers could react kicked one in the side of the head and took the other out with a right cross to the temple. They both went down in a heap.

"Go get her." Conryu removed the Cloak of Darkness and motioned Yarik toward the cabin.

He rushed through the door, but Conryu didn't follow. They deserved a moment alone together.

"You handled that well, Master," Prime said. "You're getting better at using your powers. I didn't even have to prompt you."

"I got a lot of practice this summer. Don't worry, you're not going to be out of a job any time soon."

Yarik emerged from the cabin, one arm around his wife and a suitcase in the other hand. The exhausted woman looked at Conryu and offered a shaky smile. She said something in a language he didn't recognize.

Conryu raised an eyebrow at Yarik.

"My wife thanks you for rescuing us from this hell. I thank you as well."

"My pleasure." He didn't see any reason to point out that they were about to travel through the actual Hell. "I need to cover you both in Cloak of Darkness. You might want to warn her."

Yarik babbled something at his wife who nodded. She

probably would've agreed to anything if it got her out of the Dragon Empire.

The trip back went as smoothly as he could have hoped and they emerged from the portal less than ten minutes after they left. You had to love traveling by portal.

7

THE LAND OF THE NIGHT PRINCES

Lady Wolf emerged from the portal at the exact spot she left. Her gaze darted around the empty court-yard. No unpleasant surprise waiting for her. That was a relief. Of all the things she'd expected, an attack by the witches wasn't among them. It seemed the czar intended to honor his agreement.

Anastasia must have sent them even if she didn't give a direct order. A passing comment would have been enough to encourage the overeager girls to go after them. Clearly the witches had no idea what Lady Dragon was capable of. Lady Wolf hadn't seen their temporary leader in battle for a while, but she remained every bit as impressive as she remembered. Any ambitions Lady Wolf might have harbored toward her position had died as quickly as the witches.

Lady Wolf slipped back through the door and made her way through the passages toward the Hall of Antiquities where the czar kept his baubles. Fifteen minutes from now she'd be back at headquarters, subtly letting her sisters know she'd moved a little bit ahead of them in their master's eyes. It would be fun, at least until Lady Tiger arrived with her triumph, then she'd gain pride of place, for a while. So things went in the Society.

The halls leading to her destination remained as empty now as they'd been earlier. A knot formed between Lady Wolf's shoulder blades. Something wasn't right, but unless she wanted to turn back without her prize, she had no choice but to keep going.

She reached the hall without encountering another soul. The czar stood beside the glass-enclosed case that held the artifact fragment.

He turned when she entered. "You have it?"

She took out the crystal. "As promised."

"Show me how it works."

Lady Wolf wasn't the best at light magic, but even so she should be able to manage such a simple task. Focusing her will she opened a tiny portal to Heaven and let the magic pour out. The crystal soaked up the energy like a sponge and soon it burst to life. Golden light of near-blinding intensity filled the room.

She let the light burn for a few seconds then cut off the flow. The light dimmed then vanished. "There you are. So simple even a novice at light magic could make it work. The more power you put into it, the larger the area it protects. The crystal will drain anyone using it at a rapid pace. I recommend you swap wielders every hour or two."

The czar nodded, clearly not paying her the least attention. He flicked open the case, removed the artifact fragment, and tossed it to her. It didn't look like much even up close. A

simple curved piece of metal, she didn't even know what sort –
no one did, it came from the elves' home world. You wouldn't
have guessed it had the potential to change the world, but
it did.

Lady Wolf bowed to the czar and handed him the crystal.
"If you'll excuse me, Majesty, I need to return to my order."

"I'm afraid that won't be possible, not for a little while
anyway. You'll be joining me on my campaign against the
vampires. It's not that I don't trust you regarding the crystal's
efficacy, but then again you might be lying to me. If the crystal
doesn't work as you claim, you'll share the fate of my servants."

Lady Wolf looked left and right for some means of escape.
Three wind portals opened and a trio of witches emerged,
including their leader, Anastasia. Had she been watching all
the time while she and Lady Dragon fought the witches she
sent against them? Unlikely, but not impossible.

Anastasia leaned against the czar's scale-covered chest and
smiled. "We'll be glad to have you along. You can't have too
many wizards after all."

She probably wanted another chance to reclaim the artifact
fragment. Lady Wolf had no intention of giving it to her. She'd
play along for now and bolt at the first opportunity. It wasn't
like someone could watch her every moment. There were
bound to be opportunities during a war.

"I'd be delighted to offer whatever help I can."

The czar bared his fangs. "I knew you would be."

* * *

Conryu had barely emerged from the portal when Anya
tackled him. He staggered a step then caught himself.

JAMES E WISHER

They were still alone in the rest area. Whoever owned the cars hadn't shown themselves. He looked over her head at Kai and nodded. She disappeared back into the border of Hell.

"I was so worried." Anya finally let him go. "I feared it was a trap."

"Nope, just two guys not much older than me with machine guns. After demons, dragons, and every other sort of magical threat I've dealt with over the past year they were kind of a letdown. On the other hand, it was nice to not have to fight for my life for a change."

"Excuse me, young man." Yarik gestured at the Cloak of Darkness still covering him and his wife. "Could you do something about this?"

"Sorry, I got distracted." He waved a hand, releasing the spells.

"Thank you." Yarik set his bag down and held Iliana. He murmured to her in their native language. Conryu didn't understand what they were saying, but his tone seemed to indicate genuine concern.

"Kind of sweet, aren't they?" Conryu asked.

"I'd be more gently inclined if he hadn't kidnapped me a few hours ago. So what happens now?"

"If the Department team ever arrives, we turn this lot over to them and go back to the academy. I'm sure there's plenty of cleaning up to do, though when regular classes will resume I have no idea."

"I was thinking more about what was going to happen to me. I'm not sure if I even need a bodyguard now that the people hunting me have been captured."

Conryu frowned. "That's a good thing, isn't it? I mean, it has to be a relief to know the czar's agents are under lock and key."

"It is, but now I'll be all alone." Anya hugged herself and walked a little ways away. "I don't really know anyone in this country."

"Just because I don't have to protect you every moment doesn't mean we can't be friends. You're welcome to come back with me for Christmas if you want to. Kelsie and I even worked out the sleeping arrangements."

Prime flew over and hovered a few feet above the trapped dragon-blood. The man, creature, whatever the hell it was, snarled and snapped, trying to reach the scholomantic.

"Prime! Leave the monster alone."

"Sorry, Master." Prime flew back over to Conryu. "It's just that the creature is fascinating. In all my centuries of my eternal life I've never studied such a thing up close. Do you suppose anyone would mind if we dissected it? I'd like to see if its internal structure is human or not."

"I'd mind. We're not gutting that thing on the side of the highway. Maybe if you ask nicely Malice will let you watch whatever they do to it."

"Do you think so?" Prime seemed intrigued by the idea.

Anya stared, aghast, at the two of them. Conryu sighed. "Sorry. These are the sorts of conversations you have when you hang out with a demon."

He cocked his head. In the distance the faint sounds of sirens were drawing closer. Finally, their backup. Fat lot of use they were.

Three black SUVs pulled into the rest area. Ten men with machine guns piled out along with a trio of women in gray robes. Conryu watched the men deploy with an indifferent eye. At least no one pointed a gun at him. After the day he'd had he might have gotten upset.

Two of the wizards he didn't recognize, but the withered

hag in the center he'd know anywhere, Malice Kincade. She stalked toward him, glaring at everything, especially Conryu.

She stopped and stood, knobby-knuckled hands on bony hips. "Well, what sort of trouble have you caused this time?"

Conryu gave her the condensed version. When he reached the part about going to the Empire to fetch Iliana her eyes about bugged out of her head.

"You entered a sovereign nation without permission and brought one of their citizens here? Do you have any idea what sort of a diplomatic blunder that was?"

"Considering they sent Yarik to kidnap Anya and attack the academy I can't see that they're in any position to complain. Besides, no one knows I was there."

"That's not the point! You can't just stumble along doing whatever you want without consulting with the government in Central."

"It was the right thing to do," Conryu said. As far as he was concerned nothing else mattered. "Besides, now that his wife is safe, Yarik has agreed to tell you everything he knows about the Empire. Surely a security agent can provide more information than Anya or the rebels. I also captured you a pair of dragon-men for you to play with. You should thank me."

Malice growled and waved at the still vainly struggling dragon-blood. "Bind that thing and load it in the car."

"They're resistant to magic," Conryu said.

"I don't need advice from you!" Malice glared at her subordinates who hurried over to the dragon-blood.

"Are you still mad because I wouldn't share my genetics with you?"

"Yes and don't think we've given up. Once a Kincade has made up her mind to get something, she gets it."

"Thanks for the warning. If you're done yelling at me, we need to get back to the academy."

Anya had moved a few feet away and was eavesdropping on Yarik and his wife.

"Hey, you ready to go?" Conryu asked.

"Just a second." Anya moved closer to Yarik and his wife. She asked something in Russian and Iliana responded in that language. Whatever she said caused Anya to take a step back. "Are you sure?"

"It's only a rumor," Yarik said. "The Empire is full of them."

Anya nodded and came to join Conryu who'd watched the exchange with growing confusion. "What was that about?"

"Iliana mentioned something about an invasion of the Land of the Night Princes. My mother's there."

* * *

Roman led his army through Frost Wolf Pass and into vampire country. The traveling was easy in the summer and no predator would be stupid enough to attack an army twenty thousand strong. A light breeze blew and swirled the scent of evergreen around him. Far too long had passed since Roman marched to battle with his army. He felt like a young man again, a soldier off to war.

His gaze flicked right, to the masked wizard struggling along beside him. Lady Wolf was clearly not used to walking long distances. She probably preferred to fly, but he suspected if he let her into the air, he'd never see her again. And while Roman wasn't overly concerned with the woman betraying him, he also didn't intend to die alone if the orb didn't work the way she claimed.

Speaking of the orb, at the center of the column Anastasia and her cohorts had been studying the device for the past week of their journey. She claimed to have mastered it, but the narrow-eyed looks she gave the artifact when she didn't think he was paying attention gave him pause. One way or the other they would find out soon enough. Someone had to have seen them crossing over. Word would reach Talon, and if they weren't attacked tonight, they would be tomorrow.

The army continued to march throughout the day, pausing only to eat at noon. About an hour before sunset they reached a large meadow with a brook running along the edge. It would be a perfect place to camp for the night, a perfect place to set a trap.

At Roman's command the soldiers set to work putting up their tents and lighting fires for cooking. The officers had all been briefed on their situations and tents were erected as close together as possible to minimize the area the crystal had to cover.

Lady Wolf slumped to the ground beside him drawing a chuckle from Roman. "You look weary. Perhaps marching isn't to your liking."

She turned her masked face in his direction. "I'm not one of your soldiers and marching is beneath the dignity of a wizard of my stature."

He laughed outright at that. "It's good exercise, though it would probably be easier on you if you took that mask off."

"A Society Hierarch never removes her mask when there are people around."

Roman grunted at the stupidity of that, but left the woman alone. All around the clearing everything was happening in a coordinated and efficient manner. A burst of pride struck him at the skill and professionalism of his army. The vampires would soon regret interfering in his Empire.

Before the sun even touched the horizon, the camp was nearly done. Food sizzled in pots over the flames, filling the clearing with delightful aromas. Perhaps the enemy would allow them a nice meal before attacking.

After the meal Roman was too eager to rest. He paced for a while before finally entering his tent and lying down. It wasn't that he wanted to sleep, more that the pacing seemed to make the guards nervous and hurt their focus. They needed to be sharp, especially the witches on duty.

So Roman laid awake and stared at the roof of his tent, his enhanced senses straining for any sign of the enemy's approach. The darkness presented no obstacle to his sight, not that he had much to look at.

Finally, after he knew not how long, the scuff of approaching steps reached him. Roman leapt out of bed before Anastasia even stepped through the flap.

"What is it?" he asked in a harsh whisper.

"They're coming. I can sense multiple dark auras getting closer by the moment. Shall I activate the orb?"

"Not until they're within range of its effects. This is our one chance to use it with surprise. Let's make the most of it."

"We may lose some sentries," she said.

Roman snorted. A soldier's purpose was to die for his commander. He'd gladly trade a few men for each dead vampire. "Get as many as you can."

"Understood, Majesty." Anastasia bowed and withdrew.

Now for the real test. Roman reached for the silver-coated sword sitting in the rack beside his bed. It had a wide, curved blade, perfect for chopping the heads off vampires. He'd only

killed three of the undead in his long life. The time had come
to add to his count.

Roman stepped into the meadow. He had no trouble
making out all the tents along with the guards beyond them.
The enemy was another matter. Anastasia said she sensed
them approaching, but Roman saw and felt nothing. Granted,
he wasn't as sensitive to magical energy as his witches, but he
should have seen an outline or figure or something.

A scream pierced the night followed by another and
another. Whether he saw them or not, it appeared the enemy
had arrived.

Moments after the first pained shout a blinding light filled
the clearing. Roman winced, but his eyes adjusted in seconds.
He strode toward the source of the first scream.

One of his men lay bleeding out in the grass, a rigid
vampire on either side of him. Eyes like glowing coals stared
up at the night sky. Roman moved so the undead could
see him.

"You thought you could attack me? Kill my men? No one
can resist the might of the Dragon Czar. Today you die,
again."

The silver sword went up and crashed down upon the
vampire's neck. Driven by Roman's immense strength it
cleaved through flesh and bone like it was tissue paper. The
vampire turned into black dust and blew away. He repeated
the process with the second monster and his now-dead soldier
as well, just to be safe.

From somewhere on the opposite side of the camp came a
wet thunk. One of his men must have found a target of his
own. Roman bared his fangs. Let them have a bit of fun. He
didn't want to hog it all.

"I trust you're satisfied with the artifact now?" Roman had

been so distracted by his victory he hadn't even noticed Lady Wolf's approach.

"It met my expectations. As I said, I really never doubted you, but better safe than sorry."

"May I leave now?"

"Leave? What if something goes wrong with the orb?" Roman shook his head. "I must insist you remain until the vampire's leader is dead, just to be sure."

"How long will that take?" she asked.

Roman shrugged. He was immortal, time meant little to him. Talon's head would be his, even if it took until the end of the world.

* * *

Talon licked the last of the blood from his lips and sent the elk on its way. He hadn't been able to find a boar to hunt tonight, but elk made a nice change of pace. Grazers had a mineral quality to their blood that omnivores lacked. He didn't favor it, but it wasn't unpalatable either.

He looked up at the clear, moonlit night. What should he do for amusement? Perhaps check in on the new converts. The two most recent additions to the family seemed to be settling in well, but there were always rough patches and he liked to smooth them out as much as possible. It built goodwill between him and his new subjects.

Talon smiled. Calling beings as powerful and fierce-minded as vampires his subjects might be a bit of a stretch. Perhaps first among equals would be a better description of his position. He started to dissolve into a mist when he sensed someone approaching. One of his kind rather than one of the local humans.

He solidified just as the approaching vampire arrived. Emile was a slender whip of a man, with short, slicked-back hair and narrow red eyes. "Talon. Imperials have crossed the border, an army of them. We thought to deal with them ourselves, but they have a device. It makes sunlight. We didn't stand a chance. Marius, Sveta, they killed them. I didn't know what to do."

"Slow down, Emile. The czar sent an army across the mountains? How many men?"

"A lot, fifteen, maybe twenty thousand including witches and dragon-bloods. That's not all, the czar is leading them himself. I saw Roman take Marius's head with my own eyes. If I hadn't arrived late to the battle, they would have gotten me as well."

Rage nearly choked Talon. How dare Roman enter his lands and kill his people? "Show me where."

"We can't get too close," Emile said. "The light."

"I understand. We'll keep our distance. I just want to have a look at what we're dealing with."

Emile turned into mist and led Talon north and west. They flew like the wind and after only a few minutes solidified behind a crumbled windmill well away from the gathered army.

Talon barely assumed physical form when lethargy and weakness settled over him. A hundred yards away a blinding, unnatural light revealed the sprawling enemy camp. Even so far from the source, whatever magic Roman had brought struck Talon like a physical weight.

He squinted against the glare. In half a minute Talon counted twenty witches and a hundred and fifty dragon-blood warriors. No sign of Roman. He was probably near the center of the camp. Talon had no intention of getting closer. He shuddered to think what that light might do to him if he took so much as another step nearer.

"I've seen enough," Talon said. "Let's put some distance between us and them."

Emile turned into mist before the last word fell from Talon's lips. When they'd gone twenty miles Talon resumed his physical form.

"What are we going to do?" Emile asked.

That was a good question. They couldn't confront Roman directly, not with that device protecting him. Talon racked his brain, but came up with no good options beyond avoiding the army and hoping Roman got bored and took his people home. He couldn't field an army forever, right?

Talon closed his eyes and concentrated. There weren't many of his brothers and sisters in the area, probably because Roman had already killed everyone that lived nearby. There was a small human settlement about three hours from the Imperials' position. They'd need to be evacuated before morning.

"Do you know the humans in that village?" Talon asked.

"Of course, I've whiled away many a night dancing in their tavern." Emile's narrow eyes widened. "Do you think they're in danger?"

"I'm sure of it. If Roman can't find vampires to kill, he'll certainly settle for regular people. I need you to go warn them, get the people out of there by morning and get yourself into the deepest, darkest hole you can find when the sun rises."

"What about you?"

"I need to let the elders know what has happened so they can spread the word to our people. No matter what, the Imperial army must not be approached. Go, now."

Emile vanished, leaving Talon on his own. He'd never

imagined a situation like this. In all his many years Talon had never heard of an artifact that created artificial sunlight. It was like someone designed the thing specifically to kill his kind and now it was in the hands of their most implacable enemy.

* * *

Conryu and Dean Blane stood on the shore of the lake watching the small tornado he'd conjured suck water up and shoot it into the air. A month had passed since he'd rescued Anya from Yarik and the academy had largely returned to normal, or what passed for normal at a magic school.

No one had seen their way clear to tell him what they'd done with Yarik and his wife. He hoped Malice went easy on the guy. He seemed decent enough.

Conryu twirled his finger, widening the base and transforming the water flow from a jet to a spray. He grinned. "Just like a hose nozzle."

Dean Blane nodded, but didn't reply. She stared off into space, seemingly unaware he was even there.

He snapped his fingers and the spell collapsed. "What's wrong?"

"Have you noticed anything odd about Anya? Her teachers say she's not doing very well in her classes, mind wandering, not paying attention, that sort of thing."

She'd been a little distant lately, but he figured it was shock from the attack and kidnapping so he'd given her space. Maybe he should have shown more concern.

"Want me to talk to her, see if I can get her sorted out?"

Dean Blane beamed. "Would you? I'd really appreciate it."

"Sure. Lunch is in half an hour, I'll find out what's on her mind. We going to try another spell, or do you want to call this good for today?"

She smiled, seeming back to her usual self. "How about two laps around the lake? You need to work on your precision turning."

"Race you." He shot out over the water.

To no one's great surprise he lost the race, but only by half a length. He'd gotten better in the turns, but nowhere near as good as Dean Blane. She did have thirty years' experience on him so he didn't feel too bad about it.

Conryu and Prime left the lakeshore and went to find Anya. His bodyguard duties had all but been called off so he didn't need to escort her between classes anymore. On the one hand it was a relief, on the other he now had no idea where she might be.

The cafeteria seemed as good a place as any to start so he headed that way. He pushed through the doors and found the tables half full. He spotted a few blonds, but not the one he was looking for.

"Do you see her, Prime?"

"No, Master, but your other females are trying to get your attention."

He spotted Maria waving a moment later. Kelsie sat beside her in their usual spot. Maybe one of them had seen Anya.

Maria got up as he approached and hugged him. "Are you okay? You look a little distracted."

"I'm fine. Dean Blane asked me to talk to Anya. She's been out of sorts in class lately and I'm supposed to find out why. Have you guys seen her?"

Kelsie shook her head and Maria said, "Maybe she's still in earth magic class."

"Maybe. Save us a couple spots. I'm going to keep looking."

"Good luck," Kelsie said.

He left the girls to their meals and returned to the stairs. Conryu figured she was more apt to be in her room than in class so he tried there first.

He took the steps two at a time and nearly bowled Mrs. Lenore over at the bottom. They did an awkward little dance but kept their feet.

"Sorry, you okay?" Conryu asked.

"Fine." She adjusted her robe and smoothed her hair. "What's the rush?"

"I'm trying to find Anya. Have you seen her?"

"In fact I have. We came down together. I believe she's in her room. What are you and Mrs. Umbra working on this year?"

"Wards. I mastered one that drains the life out of anyone that crosses it, leaving them unconscious but alive. It's like a fixed-position Reaper's Gale. She said if I'm stuck with the death mark I might as well learn to get the most out of it."

"I didn't know you had a death mark," Mrs. Lenore said.

Conryu rolled up the sleeve of his robe so she could see it. "I'll tell you the story sometime, but right now I need to find Anya."

"It's a date. I mean, not a date date, but you know what I mean." She trailed off in a flustered, blushing huff.

Conryu couldn't help smiling. He'd missed talking with her. "I do know what you mean. And it is a date. See you later."

He left the still-crimson-cheeked teacher in the hall and made the short walk to Anya's room. He knocked and waited. When no one responded he tried again. Still nothing.

"Is she in there?"

"Someone is," Prime said. "I assume it's her."

"Anya? It's Conryu. Can we talk?"

Another minute passed and he was just about to knock down the door when it finally opened. Anya looked at him with dark, bloodshot eyes. Her robe looked like she'd been sleeping in it. "Sorry. I thought you were that teacher. She's sweet, but kind of annoying. Come in."

He stepped inside. Her room looked like one of his twisters had hit it. Clothes lay everywhere and she hadn't made the bed.

"So what's up?" He sat in the room's only chair and faced the bed.

"Nothing." She flopped on the mattress and stared at the ceiling. Talk about not convincing.

"Come on, something's bothering you. Dean Blane says you've been spacing out in class and it doesn't look like you've been sleeping."

She sat up. "I'm worried about my mom. I can't stop thinking about what Iliana said about the czar going to war with the vampires. She could be fighting for her life right now and there's nothing I can do about it. It's so frustrating."

"Why didn't you say something? If you want to go see your mom, I'll take you."

She stared at him for a moment. "You will?"

"Sure, we can go by dark portal on Sunday. I don't have anything better to do with Maria buried up to her eyeballs in alchemy books. Besides, if I'm gone Kelsie can't get me to test her cooking. We'll need to figure out what time the sun sets over there. No sense arriving before your mom's out of bed. You can check in and we'll be back before anyone knows we're gone."

Anya leapt off the bed and hugged him. "Thank you, I feel better already. I can't wait to see her. I'm sure she'll be keen to meet you too."

"Cool. I've never talked to a vampire. It'll be a good one to knock off my list."

* * *

Conryu sat at the desk in his room and paged through the wind magic notes Dean Blane had given him, not really seeing the words. Sunday had arrived and after a nice lunch with Maria he'd retreated to his room to prepare. In a few hours they'd be leaving for the Land of the Night Princes. Anya wanted to go to the port of Constanta since she'd last seen her mother there. That suited Conryu, he considered himself more of a chauffeur than anything on this trip.

He gave up and tossed his notebook on the desk. "Hey Prime, what do you know about vampires?"

"A great deal, Master. What would you like me to tell you?"

"How do I protect myself from them? Anya says they're friendly, but I'd rather not go in without a backup plan."

"A wise precaution, Master. Vampires are essentially humans that have swapped the light energy that animated them for dark. The energy transformation grants them certain powerful magical abilities, but leaves them vulnerable to sunlight and silver, both of which are associated with light magic. They can also be controlled by powerful dark magic."

"Like what I did with the demons?"

"Exactly. Demons and vampires aren't that different. A demon is dark magic given physical form and a vampire is a physical form filled with dark magic. You shouldn't have any difficulty controlling one or the other."

"Do I use the domination spell?" As long as he didn't have to fight a crowd of them all at once he should be okay.

"There's a variation of it that might work better." Prime flipped open and flew down into his hands.

Conryu read the spell over and over until he had it committed to memory. It really was a minor variation. Since his will controlled the magic he could probably get by with the demon version, but then again why risk it.

Kai emerged from Hell and bowed. "I don't believe this is a wise move, Chosen. Let me return home and gather a proper guard detail for you."

"Your dark weapons would be of little use against vampires," Prime said.

Kai rested her hand on the hilt of her sword and glared at the scholomantic.

"Easy, you two. We're not going to fight, just to say hi to Anya's mom. She said she knows their leader so we should be fine. That said, I'm glad to have you as my ace in the hole, Kai."

"You may depend on me, Chosen." She bowed again and vanished.

"Are you trying to get yourself cut in half?" Conryu asked.

"What? I simply wished to point out that her weapons may be less than effective against these particular enemies. I meant no offense."

"Try to be more careful in the future. Kai seems a little touchy when it comes to her weapons skills."

Prime snorted, an astonishing noise coming from a book. "You humans are so hard to predict. What sets off one of you doesn't bother another in the least. Demons seem almost easy to predict in comparison."

"Sure, demons want to kill you no matter what you say."

"Exactly."

A quick knock ended their conversation. Before he could even get out of his chair Anya opened the connecting door and entered his room. She'd changed out of her robes and into a flowing white dress that left her legs bare from mid-thigh. A gold cross with a ruby in the center rested on her chest.

"Nice outfit. Are you ready to go?"

"Yup. I wore a dress like this the day we had to leave our house. I thought Mom might be more likely to remember me." She chewed her lip a moment then asked, "You don't think she'll have forgotten, do you? You know, because of the transformation."

Conryu couldn't imagine anyone forgetting Anya once they got a look at her. Before he could offer reassurance Prime said, "Do not be concerned. Though the change from human to vampire can be traumatic, it doesn't cause any damage to the transformed person's brain. Assuming your mother had no memory issues while alive, she shouldn't have any now."

Anya nodded and from her expression he figured she didn't know whether to be reassured or not. A fairly typical reaction whenever Prime said something.

"We can stand here worrying about it or go see for ourselves." Conryu held out his hand and when Anya took it he cast, "Cloak of Darkness." Dark magic covered her from head to toe, protecting her from exposure to the energy of Hell.

"Feels a little cool," Anya said.

"It won't be for long. Reveal the way through infinite darkness. Open the path. Hell Portal!"

The portal opened and Conryu pulled her through. It had barely closed behind them when Cerberus appeared.

Anya yelped and moved behind him. Another typical reaction. At least the demon dog didn't feel the need to growl at her.

Conryu patted him on the flank. "Good boy. Wanna go for a run?"

Cerberus barked and danced in a circle. Conryu couldn't help smiling whenever he saw the giant demon hound prancing like a puppy. He looked around for Kai, but if the ninja was nearby, she kept herself well hidden.

"Prime, how do I say 'Constanta' in Infernal?"

"It doesn't translate. Don't worry. Just focus on where you want to go and Cerberus will get us there."

"Cool." At Conryu's mental command they flew up and landed on Cerberus's back. He started to warn Anya to hold on, but the moment they settled in place she grabbed him around the waist so tight he had a little trouble breathing. "Okay, pal. Constanta, let's go."

Cerberus barked and they were off.

* * *

Conryu couldn't recall ever seeing a more bleak landscape than the docks of Constanta. It looked like someone had bombed the place to ruins. The burned-out shells of half a dozen buildings sat to their left while to the right was the shell of an abandoned fortress. The sun hadn't fully set yet, but he didn't see any good place for a vampire to spend the night.

"It's all different," Anya said as she turned in a circle. "The docks were run down before, but nothing like this. The vampires lived in those warehouses, or they were living there when we arrived. I'm not sure what we should do."

"Prime? Do you sense anything?"

"No vampires, Master, but I detect a handful of humans."

Conryu deepened his connection with Prime to get an idea what he felt. The faint life forces came from their right, toward the main part of the city. He sensed nothing remarkable about them.

"Scavengers, you think?" Neither Prime nor Anya had any idea, so he turned toward the city. "Let's have a look around. Maybe someone can point us in the right direction."

"Do you even speak the local language?" Prime asked.

Conryu stopped in his tracks. "Good point. Anya? Do the locals speak your language?"

"The ones I dealt with spoke English. Still, there's a lot of cross-border smuggling with the Empire so I'll bet we can find someone that'll understand us."

That was good enough for Conryu. They set off again, following Prime toward the life forces he sensed.

The sun had fully set when they reached the city proper, forcing him to conjure a light. Steel and glass towers rose far above them. It didn't look that different from Sentinel City or Central aside from the scale, assuming you could overlook the complete lack of people. The total silence seemed foreign to such a cosmopolitan area. It was like walking through a giant tomb. Not at all inappropriate given the local rulers.

"It doesn't seem like we're getting any closer," Conryu said.

"Perhaps whoever lives here doesn't wish to be found," Anya said. She hugged herself and shivered. The thin dress probably wasn't warm enough in the cool evening.

"Master!"

Conryu heard the steps a moment after Prime's warning. He spun in time to see a man emerge from a side street. He had a long, curved dagger bare in his hand.

Five steps from them a shapely, black-clad leg appeared from out of nowhere and kicked him under the chin. The attacker went down like a ton of bricks and stayed there when Kai's sword touched his throat.

Conryu could have handled a single assailant on his own, but he appreciated Kai stepping in. That's what a ninja body-guard was for after all.

"Who might you be then?" Conryu asked.

The man offered nothing beyond a low growl. Not at all friendly.

"You might want to drop that knife," Conryu said. "You're making Kai nervous."

Kai cocked her head. "I'm not nervous, Chosen. If he does anything I don't like I can kill him with a flick of my wrist. Rest assured he poses no danger to anyone now."

"I stand corrected. Anya, do you have any questions for the knife-wielding maniac?"

"Where are the vampires? I need to find my mom."

The man glared at them then said in clear if heavily accented English, "Do your worst, Imperial. You'll get nothing from me."

Conryu and Anya shared a look.

"We're not from the Empire," Conryu said. "Well, I suppose Anya technically is, but she ran away. She passed through this country on her way and her mom was injured and trans-formed into a vampire. We're just here to check in. Honest."

He looked closer at them. When his gaze landed on Anya his eyes widened.

"That cross, may I see it?" he asked.

Kai pressed the tip of her sword to the soft flesh under his chin drawing a pained hiss. "The prisoner doesn't get to make requests. If you refuse to answer the Chosen's questions you will prove yourself worthless and thus expendable."

"It's okay." Anya crouched down. "Lord Talon gave this to me just before I left. He said anyone that saw it would know not to harm me."

"I thought I recognized it. I've seen the master wearing that cross before. When I asked him about it once he said it amused him to wear something humans imagined should cause him pain. I apologize for attacking you, but I believed you were Imperial scouts."

"Don't trust him, Chosen," Kai said.

"I agree." Prime flew down so he was just a few feet above the man. "Perhaps she should remove his knife hand. I'm curious to see how that sword cuts."

"That's a reasonable idea," Kai said. "If we remove his weapon hand, the risk will be greatly diminished."

Conryu slapped his palm to his forehead. "Right. This guy works for the head vampire. Maiming him would be a great way to make a first impression. Prime, give the man some breathing room. Kai, you can watch him, but no cutting unless he attacks one of us. Got it?"

"Fine." Prime flew up away from the prisoner, sulking through their link.

"As you wish, Chosen." Kai took her blade from his throat. "I will be watching closely."

"Okay, fine. Now, Mr...?"

"Xavier." The man climbed to his feet and sheathed his knife. "I answer directly to Lord Talon. He ordered me to keep watch on the port in case the Imperials tried to establish a second front in the invasion."

"So it's true," Anya said. "We've heard rumors. Is everyone okay?"

"Unfortunately, no. Twenty vampires have been killed so far that I know about. The bastards have a weapon that renders them immobile even at night. We can't counterattack and every day they send out hunters to find sleeping vampires. At the rate things are going..." Xavier shook his head. "Follow

140

me. I have a radio at my camp. We'll contact Lord Talon and see what he wants to do."

"Lead on," Conryu said. He'd really hoped the rumor of an invasion would turn out to be nothing. He should have known better. The one rule of his life was that anything that could go wrong would.

8

A BAD SITUATION

Xavier had his base – if you could call a sleeping bag, camp stove, and radio a base – in the half-finished fort. He led Conryu and the others there at the tip of Kai's sword. Despite his repeated assurances she didn't put the weapon away. While Conryu appreciated her concern, it was possible to take it too far.

She backed off when Xavier sat down in front of the radio and switched it on. It crackled to life and he said, "This is Xavier making contact from Constanta. Lord Talon, are you there?"

The silence dragged for half a minute when someone replied, "I hear you. Have the Imperials attempted to return?"

"No, my lord. I have guests. Anya Kazakov and a friend. She says she knows you and has your gold cross to prove it. The girl wishes to see her mother who I gather is one of the new converts."

"I hadn't thought to see her again so soon, but she's certainly welcome. I can be there with her mother in an hour."

Conryu shook his head. "No need. If he provides a location, I can take us there in moments."

"Our guests request permission to come to you, my lord."

"That would be most convenient. We're holed up in a small city seven hundred and fifty miles northwest of Constanta. Is that sufficient?"

Xavier looked at Conryu who nodded.

"That's fine, my lord. I'll send them on their way. Out." Xavier switched off the radio. "May I be of any further assistance before you leave?"

"No, thank you," Conryu said. "You're welcome to join us if you like."

"My assignment is here." Xavier bowed to Anya. "I hope you find your mother well."

"Thank you."

Conryu led the group out of the fort. Kai finally put her sword away and vanished without a word. Xavier raised an eyebrow. "You keep interesting company."

Conryu grinned and thought of the Dark Lady and Cerberus. "You have no idea. Stay safe. Reveal the way through infinite darkness. Open the path. Hell Portal!"

The disk opened and they stepped through.

An instant later Conryu, Anya, and Prime emerged at the edge of a park with a dry fountain. The vampires he'd seen through his viewing window had vanished when they arrived. He frowned at the unfriendly greeting. They'd been invited after all.

He shrugged and conjured a light. "They're your friends. Maybe you should say something."

"Lord Talon?" Anya said. "Mom? Is anyone here?"

A tall, pale figure detached himself from the darkness. He

was dressed in an all-black suit and his eyes burned red in the dark. Conryu tensed, but Anya smiled.

"Lord Talon. It's good to see you again." She showed him the cross around her neck. "I wore it like you said."

Finally the vampire smiled. "So you did. I apologize for the less-than-friendly welcome. We have to take precautions given our precarious position."

"I heard about the invasion," Anya said. "That's why I came. I wanted to make sure Mom was okay."

"She is. I sent word for her to join us. I've made every effort to keep the younger members of our family far from the enemy. While we wait perhaps you can introduce me to your companion."

Anya blushed. "I'm sorry. Lord Talon, this is Conryu Koda. He's been generous enough to protect me from some of the Empire's agents."

"The boy wizard. A pleasure, young man." Lord Talon held out his hand and Conryu gave it a shake. "No hesitation about shaking hands with a vampire?"

Conryu grinned. "No, sir. Some of my best friends are demons – the ill-mannered book floating at my shoulder, for example. Shaking hands with a vampire doesn't even make my top five list of weird things. I must admit I'm surprised you've heard of me out here."

"We may be isolated, but some news still reaches us. I would have had to be living at the bottom of the deepest mine not to have heard of you."

Conryu grimaced. "Yeah. So what's the deal with the Imperials?"

Before Lord Talon could answer a sultry female voice said, "Kiska?"

"Mom!" Anya looked around trying to spot her.

A woman in black emerged from the darkness. She could have been Anya's sister, same blond hair, same amazing figure. The only difference was the eyes. They were blood red.

* * *

"Kiska?" No one else in the whole world called Anya that.

"Mom?"

A female vampire formed out of the darkness just like Lord Talon. It was her mother and at the same time it wasn't. The fine wrinkles had vanished along with the hint of gray in her hair. She appeared to have reverse-aged twenty years.

But the eyes were what really startled her. The burning, blood-red pits glowing in her mother's youthful face hammered home that this was both her mother and not. Mom smiled, revealing her elongated eye teeth.

"I've missed you so, kiska."

She opened her arms and Anya hugged her. The embrace grew tighter and tighter until Anya groaned. "Too tight. Can't breathe."

"Sorry, sweetheart. I haven't gotten full control over my powers yet. Lord Talon says it can take years."

"Decades in some cases." Lord Talon joined them along with Conryu. "Sasha is a quick study. She can already dematerialize at will."

She seemed unimpressed with the compliment. Instead, her gaze was locked on Conryu. "Who is this handsome man?"

"Conryu Koda, Mrs. Kazakov." Conryu held out his hand.

Her mother took a hold and seemed to make a conscious

effort not to squeeze too tight. She also made no effort to let go. When Mom licked her lips in an entirely inappropriate way Anya said, "Conryu's been helping me out as a bodyguard. He handled the transportation here too."

"How versatile. What else can he do?" Mom purred and moved closer to Conryu who did his best to keep the space between them.

"Mom!" Anya's cheeks burned. What in the world was wrong with her mother?

She finally took her eyes off Conryu and pouted. "Don't you want to share, kiska? It's rude to keep such a lovely boy all to yourself."

"Oh my god, Mom."

Lord Talon swept in and separated Conryu and her mother. "Sasha, we talked about this. You need to control your urges."

"But he's so yummy." She licked her lips again and Conryu took a quick step back, his gaze darting all over the place in search of an escape route.

Anya had never been so embarrassed in her life, yet she didn't dare say much about it since she was the one that agreed to let her mother be transformed into what she was now. "What happened to you?"

"Your mother is fine," Lord Talon said. "Hypersexuality is a common side effect of the transformation. Her senses have been heightened and everything she experiences has more impact. In a year or two she'll get used to it and return to normal, more or less. Why don't you two go get reacquainted? I'll keep Conryu company."

"That's a great idea!" Conryu flicked his wrist and the glowing orb over his head flew to her. "There you go. You two have fun."

"Isn't he cute?" Mom said.

Anya grabbed her arm and dragged her what she hoped was a safe distance away. They found a park bench and sat.

Now that they were alone Anya wasn't sure what to say. Finally she blurted out, "I'm sorry. When I thought you were going to die, I couldn't stand it. I accepted Lord Talon's offer on your behalf. I know it wasn't my place..."

Her mother placed a finger over her lips. "It's okay, Anya. I'm glad to still be alive, or at least reasonably alive. I would have made the same choice for another chance to see you. I don't regret what happened and neither should you. Perhaps when you get older, you'll join me. Assuming those bastards from the Empire don't kill us all first."

"Is it that bad?"

"Bad enough. Not many have been destroyed, but that's only because we spend so much time putting distance between us and the army every night then we sleep in the deepest niches of the earth, ones that can only be accessed by someone able to dematerialize. Even so, it's only a matter of time before the witches figure out some way to find us and dig us out. Or just wait until the thirst drives us to the surface where they can kill us."

"If there's anything I can do, I'll do it. I can shoot. I... I even killed a man in Paris."

Mom put an arm around her and pulled her close. "I love you, kiska."

"I love you too." Why did it feel so much like a goodbye when she said it?

* * *

I t was with considerable relief that Conryu watched Anya and her mother move out into the night. He conjured a second light sphere so he wouldn't be left in the dark. They'd probably be a while, so he looked around for somewhere to sit.

"I hope Sasha wasn't too hard on you," Lord Talon said.

"Nah, though it's a good thing my girlfriend is half a world away otherwise she'd be strangling me right now." Conryu settled on the edge of the fountain as his best option.

Talon laughed, a surprisingly human sound. "You're handling this better than most humans would. Anya, I can understand. She's spent time with us before, but you treat chatting with me like it's the most normal thing in the world."

"I've been marked by the Reaper, nearly killed by the Devil, stepped into a portal to the netherworld twice, and made more trips through Hell than I care to count. Hanging out with a vampire practically is normal for me."

"Pity more humans aren't equally open-minded." Talon settled in beside him. "Given our nature, we have limited contact with other nations and we only have good relations with Germany, since they're on our western border."

"If you're waiting for humans to make sense, it's a good thing vampires live forever."

Talon tensed and a moment later another vampire solidified before them, a young-looking man with a gaunt build. "Lord Talon, some of the humans are under attack by the enemy army."

Talon bared his fangs. "Do they have the artifact?"

"I didn't see it, but I didn't get close either. What should we do?"

Talon leapt to his feet and paced. It seemed like an easy decision to Conryu, but then he wasn't the one at risk of getting paralyzed and killed. Wait, the artifact posed no danger to him. Maybe he could help.

"How many soldiers are we talking about?" Conryu asked.

"Who are you?" The newcomer glared at him with glowing eyes.

"Conryu is my guest," Talon said. "You will address him with the proper respect, Horatio."

The vampire lowered his gaze. "My apologies. There are around three hundred soldiers with perhaps fifty families trapped. I saw no witches or dragon-bloods."

"Arrogant bastard!" Talon said. "Roman would never have dared send such a weak force before he gained his new weapon."

"Sounds like a trap," Conryu said. "How much do you want to bet there's a witch hiding in whatever elemental realm she's aligned to, just waiting to spring out and paralyze any of you that shows up?"

"That's exactly the sort of thing Roman would try. If I send some of my people to help the humans, he kills vampires and if I don't he kills the humans. Either way Roman wins."

"What's going on?" Anya asked as she and her mother came to join the conversation. Sasha gave him one long look, but she seemed to have herself better under control now.

"Another Imperial raid. We were discussing our options, but none of them are good." Talon's dejection came through loud and clear. Clearly being helpless wasn't something the vampire was used to.

"I can try to rescue them if you'd like," Conryu said.

Horatio barked a laugh. "What hope could a single human have?"

Conryu grinned. "I know a few tricks. I don't want to stick

my nose in where it doesn't belong, but innocent people getting killed sits poorly with me."

"With me as well," Talon said. "Do what you can. Where are they, Horatio?"

"An old church of St. Simon about four hundred miles west of here. The stone walls are slowing the attack since the Imperials didn't bring heavy weapons."

"Definitely a trap." Conryu got up. "Where should I send them? I can't bring that many people through a Hell portal."

"Send them east," Talon said. "Horatio will meet them two miles from the church and guide them somewhere safe – safer anyway."

Conryu nodded and gathered his will.

"Wait!" Anya ran over and grabbed his arm. "You can't fight that many soldiers on your own, you'll be killed."

"Thanks for the vote of confidence."

"Don't joke. This isn't your fight and these aren't your people. Why risk it?"

All three vampires were staring at him now. Conryu grimaced a moment then decided the simplest explanation would be best. "I'm doing it for the same reason I agreed to help you and rescue Iliana: it's the right thing."

He eased his arm free of her grasp and chanted, "Reveal the way through infinite darkness. Open the path. Hell Portal!"

When the portal had closed behind them Prime asked, "Do you have a plan?"

"Of course I have a plan, sort of. Can I cast a spell through a portal without actually leaving Hell?"

"No, Master. Magic doesn't work through portals that way."

"Naturally, that would've been too easy. Okay, Plan B. I appear behind the soldiers and cast Reaper's Grasp. With my new power boost it should take out that many soldiers, right?"

"It'll be tricky," Prime said. "You'll need to cast it at full power, but diffuse the energy so no single soldier gets hit too hard, otherwise…"

"Otherwise I'll end up with a pile of corpses. Which would probably please the Reaper no end."

"Precisely."

Cerberus trotted up and gave a happy bark. His guardian demon seemed pleased by the extra time Conryu had been spending in Hell lately. He leapt onto the demon dog's back and they were off.

It didn't take more than a few seconds to reach the proper location. Conryu opened a vision gate revealing a tumbled-down stone church getting pelted with bullets from three different positions, fortunately all on the same side of the church.

He maneuvered around until he stood about a hundred yards away from the nearest position and generally in line with the other two. He took a deep, steadying breath and opened a portal.

The moment he emerged he cast, "Fingers of the Reaper, black and twisted. Reach for my enemies and claw the life from them. Feed me their souls that I may be strong, Reaper's Grasp!"

Guided by his will, scores of dark spirits poured from Conryu and flew out into the gathered soldiers. He focused every bit of mental energy he could muster to command them not to kill anybody. The first one returned mere seconds later and filled him with energy. He'd cast quite a few powerful spells tonight and the recharge felt amazing.

Conryu didn't let the energy infusion distract him. He also didn't let the screaming dissuade him. A few soldiers tried to shoot the bodiless spirits, but they might better have saved their bullets.

Two minutes later all was silent. No witch appeared, whether because there wasn't one watching or because she didn't detect any vampires, he couldn't say.

The final spirit returning to him paused before Conryu. "Did you enjoy your feast?" the Reaper's cold voice asked.

"Not especially," Conryu said. It was partly a lie, but he'd never admit to enjoying the sensation of stolen life energy entering his body. "Thanks for the power boost."

"One day, boy, your focus will slip, just a tiny bit, and I will have a feast of my own." The spirit vanished without delivering its load of energy.

"Do you think that means I managed not to kill anyone?"

"I believe it does, Master."

Thank goodness for small favors.

* * *

Conryu watched the sun rise from five thousand feet in the air. After last night's successful rescue, he'd earned the respect of Horatio and Talon. When he offered to help them with their Imperial problem, the vampire lord had been quick to accept.

While the vampires slept, Conryu intended to take a quick look at the opposition. Anya had offered to join him, but she looked exhausted after the long night and besides he didn't know how to carry someone with him when he flew yet. Conryu was still buzzed from the infusion of life energy, so he and Prime set out at first light.

The army hadn't been hard to find; it sprawled over the equivalent of four football fields. He didn't see much activity considering the size of the force. Being on alert all night must have tired them out. Good for Conryu. He was way less likely to be noticed this way.

"You'll need more than a Reaper's Grasp to deal with that many people," Prime said.

"No kidding."

Conryu cast the farseeing spell Terra had taught him and took a closer look. The tents looked to be in good shape. Small groups of men with rifles slung over their shoulders marched around the perimeter of the camp looking more bored than alert. No need to be too cautious when your main enemy slept all day.

He shifted his gaze toward the center of the tents. *Hello, what have we here?* At his mental command the view zoomed in closer. A woman dressed in a fur-trimmed gray robe, wearing a mask that resembled a dog stalked along looking like she wanted to kill someone.

What was a Le Fay Society member doing mixed up with an army? Were they allied or was she a mercenary? Or maybe she'd provided them with this new weapon. That struck him as very likely. Why the Society would provide the Dragon Czar with such a valuable item was something he very much wanted to know.

"Master!"

Conryu ended the spell and focused on his link with Prime to see what had the scholomantic upset. A figure in white was flying toward them like a bullet. Seemed they'd been spotted.

He blasted away from the camp in the opposite direction from the vampire's base. The last thing he wanted was to lead the witch back to Anya and the defenseless Sasha.

A bolt of lightning streaked by, close enough to singe the

hair from his arm. If she wanted to play rough, he'd be happy to oblige.

He pulled up and spun.

A blur of white shot by.

He raised a hand. "Break!"

A sphere of dark magic streaked after the witch. Guided by his will, it followed her every move like a heat-seeking missile.

Finally she hurled a lightning bolt at it and the two magics canceled each other out. Pretty impressive.

Conryu put his hands together. "Darkness dispels everything."

Dark energy gathered between his palms.

The witch gathered herself for another spell. Power crackled around her hands.

Conryu finished first. He hurled the ball of energy at her.

It exploded, dispelling all magic in a thirty-foot area.

The witch plummeted toward the ground.

He opened a Hell portal and watched just long enough to make sure she caught herself before throwing a little wave her way and flying through the portal.

* * *

A shiver ran up Lady Wolf's spine as she stalked around the quiet camp. She'd already wasted a month with these Imperial fools and the operation showed no sign of coming to an end any time soon. Did the czar really expect her to spend months on end doing nothing at his side while he hunted vampires? Surely by this point the Solar Orb had proven its usefulness. It should be clear to anyone with half a brain that she'd held up her side of the deal.

It was probably some sort of power play. He wanted to

prove he possessed strength enough to force her to do what he wanted. A month should have been enough to satisfy this. She paused and looked up into the clear sky. Unfortunately, no solution presented itself.

A hint of movement caught her eye. The dot soon resolved into a witch approaching at high speed. She flew straight for the czar's huge tent. Eager for anything to alleviate her boredom, Lady Wolf followed.

She reached the tent just as the witch touched down. The flap opened before the witch could take a single step closer and the czar emerged. He must have been able to sense her anxiety through the link that allowed him to control them.

"What has happened?" he asked.

"A spy was surveying the camp from a distance. I drove him off, but I don't know what he might have seen."

Lady Wolf frowned behind her mask. No vampire would be out flying at this time of day. A sick feeling twisted her stomach.

"Did you get a good look at this spy?" the czar asked.

"Not too good. It was a young man dressed in black. He escaped through a Hell portal or else I would have captured him."

"A man, able to fly, you're certain?" Roman scratched his chin with a long talon.

"Yes, Majesty. Though I sensed no device powering the spells."

"Of course not," Lady Wolf said. "You had the dubious pleasure of meeting Conryu Koda, the only male wizard on earth. The abomination has been a thorn in our side since his discovery."

"You seem familiar with this boy," the czar said.

"I've never encountered him personally, but he ruined one

of our projects this past summer. I recommend you withdraw back to the Empire before he does to you what he did to us."

Roman laughed. "You expect me to lead my army away because a single whelp of a wizard has arrived on the battle-field? Surely you're joking."

"I assure you I'm serious. If the abomination has allied with the vampires, your chances of victory have just dropped by more than half. You've sent a message, killed some enemies, showed them they can't interfere with you and get away with it. Take the win and walk away. That's my advice."

Roman's eyes glowed as he scowled at her. "And let you return to your precious Society? Your motives are painfully transparent. We're not going anywhere, and neither are you."

The czar returned to his tent, ending the conversation. Lady Wolf silently cursed the arrogant fool. Yes, she would have liked to take her leave of the Empire, but that in no way lessened the risk of having Conryu on the battlefield. His power alone sufficed to change the shape of the war. And if he somehow found out her plans or worse captured her and the artifact fragment, all hope of freeing Morgana would vanish. She couldn't have that. Nothing could be allowed to interfere with her mission.

* * *

Maria sat at the end of their usual table and picked at her salad. She hadn't seen Conryu since Sunday and she was getting worried. Especially since Anya had gone missing as well. She didn't believe for a second he'd run off with the beautiful girl. He wasn't that sort of person. No, she could definitely rule out them going off together.

The slightly more worrying idea that wouldn't stop

gnawing at the back of her brain was that the Department had sent him off on some new, dangerous mission. Her father, or more likely Malice Kincade, might have ordered him not to say anything to her or anyone else. She tried to imagine what they might have sent him to do, but the options were too vast. Whenever the Department had a difficult problem, it seemed they looked to Conryu as their first and only option.

She tossed her fork on the plate and ground her teeth. Whether he was in danger or not, the not knowing bothered her more than anything.

"Have you seen him?" Kelsie sat beside her and tapped her finger on the table.

"No. I don't suppose you heard anything through your family?"

Kelsie shook her head. "No one talks to me anymore. I prefer that most of the time, but right now it would be nice to have those connections. What are we going to do?"

"I've got a free period after lunch," Maria said. "I'll go see Dean Blane and find out if she knows what's going on."

"I'll go too. I have light magic class, but I'm not progressing enough to make it worthwhile."

Maria reached out and stilled her tapping finger. "Maybe it would be best if just one of us goes. We don't want to act like we're making demands. As soon as I hear anything, I'll let you know."

Kelsie scrunched up her face and Maria feared she might argue. After a moment Kelsie sighed. "Promise?"

Maria made a little *X* over her heart. "Promise."

Maria left the cafeteria and made the short walk over to the main building. Upstairs in the administrative area all the damage from the dragon mane had been repaired and all the secretaries had returned to work.

It never ceased to amaze her, the things you could accomplish with magic. Maria ignored the looks from the secretaries and marched straight down to the dean's office. She knocked and the door opened almost at once.

Dean Blane sat behind her desk, a worried crease in her otherwise youthful face. Before Maria could get a word out the dean asked, "Do you know where he's gotten to?"

Maria's heart sank. Dean Blane didn't know either. That made the Department sending him off on a mission much less likely.

"I was hoping you did. The last time I saw Conryu was Sunday at lunch. Since then it's like he vanished off the face of the earth." Her eyes widened. "That's not possible, is it?"

"With that boy I hesitate to say anything's impossible, but it is very unlikely." Dean Blane hopped off her chair and came around her desk. "I guess we'll have to look for him."

Maria brightened. "Do you think you can find him?"

"Of course. Wind wizards are the best at this sort of thing. If the air is touching him, the spirits can find him, especially since I haven't taught him how to hide from them yet."

A wave of her hand and one of the bookcases slid aside revealing a mirror. Dean Blane chanted in the language of air and clouds filled the glass. She frowned and stared, starting the clouds swirling. Maria didn't know much about scrying and dearly wanted to ask questions, but she knew better than to distract a wizard in the middle of a spell.

It took most of half an hour for the clouds to part and reveal Conryu sitting on a rusty park bench alone in a clearing. He had Prime in his hands and appeared deep in thought.

"Where is he?" Maria asked.

"I'm not exactly sure, the spirits aren't fantastic when it comes to human ideas like boundaries and nations. Considering the setting and how long it took to find him I'd guess Europe somewhere. The more pressing question is: What the hell is he doing there instead of here?"

"Can't we ask him?"

"We certainly can. And he'd better have a good explanation."

Dean Blane chanted again and Conryu looked up from Prime and straight at them. He offered a sheepish wave.

"Well, what do you have to say for yourself?" Dean Blane asked.

"I find I'm in a bit of a complicated situation. Remember how you said you wanted me to find out what was bothering Anya and try to fix it?"

"Yeah."

"Turns out she was worried about her mom, so I offered to take her for a visit. It was supposed to be just for a night and we'd be back this morning for class, but I ran into a problem."

"What kind of problem?" the dean asked.

"The Dragon Empire has invaded and they're hunting vampires." Maria's heart skipped a beat, but Conryu went right on talking. "Apparently they've got an elf artifact that creates artificial sunlight and they're powerless to deal with it on their own. The Imperial soldiers are also killing any regular people they run into. I rescued a group of fifty families last night. Must've been sixty kids with the group and the soldiers were shooting at them with machine guns."

"This isn't your fight," Dean Blane said. "If the Alliance government knew you'd gotten involved in a foreign war, they'd lose their minds. You need to grab Anya and get back here right now."

Conryu stared at them through the mirror and Maria steeled herself. She'd seen that expression before and if there were innocent people in danger, it wouldn't matter to him where they lived. He wasn't coming back, at least not soon.

"I already volunteered to help them out and the vampire's leader accepted. There's another thing I forgot to mention. The Imperials have a Le Fay Society member with them and I'd bet my bike she's the one that provided them with the artifact."

Dean Blane's expression shifted to one of concern. "Why would the Society be helping the Empire?"

"Exactly what I'm hoping to find out. Whatever it is, I doubt it's good for us or anyone else. Can't you cover for me until we get this straightened out? I already know enough spells to pass the midterm so that won't be a problem. Besides, I doubt Anya would leave with her mother in danger, I certainly wouldn't."

Dean Blane sighed and Maria knew he'd won. "Alright, we'll keep things quiet here. It'll help that you're not in any formal classes. Is there anything we can do?"

"Anything you can find out about an artifact that creates artificial sunlight would be great. Prime's teaching me how to switch it off, but his knowledge of light-magic-based items is very limited."

Prime grumbled something, but Maria couldn't make it out. Conryu shooed him away.

"I'll speak to St. Seraphim, she's our expert. Give me a few hours and I'll be back in touch."

"Sure, my hosts won't wake up until sunset anyway."

"Please, be careful," Maria said before Dean Blane could sever the connection.

He grinned. "I'll be fine. Love you."

"Love you too."

The image vanished and Dean Blane waved the bookcase

back into place. "I trust I don't need to tell you not a word of this leaves my office."

"I have to tell Kelsie, she's nearly frantic."

"Her and no one else. If Malice got wind of Conryu's shenanigans she'd have him locked up before you could say civil rights."

Maria nodded. She couldn't even begin to guess how Conryu would react if someone tried to arrest him for helping people. The only certain thing was it would be ugly.

* * *

"Are you sure just my regular dispel won't work?" Conryu had been studying the page on a spell called Focused Dispel for the past hour and change. He understood the basic concept, but risking everything on a spell he'd never cast before seemed unwise.

Prime flew up out of his hands. "An elf artifact is by a large margin the most powerful magic you've ever tried to dispel. It's possible your spell would succeed, but the chances are it wouldn't. Focused Dispel gathers that huge sphere of dark magic and compresses it into a narrow area, giving the maximum chance for success. I assure you I wouldn't lead you astray."

"I know you wouldn't, pal. Let's run through it once more. I cast my normal dispel then instead of releasing it I compress it between my palms and focus only on the crystal. If it works right, I should get a line of energy instead of an explosion. Right?"

"Exactly, Master. I have every confidence in your ability to pull it off."

"Thanks, Prime."

Anya emerged from the ruined building serving as their hotel, her hair in disarray, rubbing sleep from her eyes. She spotted him and stifled a yawn. "Did you get any sleep?"

"Just a quick cat nap. I'm still buzzed from the life energy I got yesterday. Dean Blane got in touch."

Anya winced. "How mad is she?"

"Less mad than worried. We're in the middle of a war zone after all." Conryu glanced at the sky. The horizon had begun turning pink and purple. Wouldn't be long now before the others got up. "Is there anything to eat around here? I'd love a Giovanni's pizza."

"I don't think so." Anya sat beside him on the bench he'd appropriated. "I really appreciate you doing this for my mom and everyone."

"My pleasure, though your mom makes me a little nervous, and not because she's a vampire."

"Yeah, she's different than I expected, but she's still Mom."

The last of the light vanished and black mist rose out of the ground. Soon Sasha and Talon arrived.

"Morning," Conryu said. "Or I guess evening. I don't mean to be rude, but where can a guy get a bite to eat around here?"

"I don't have anything handy, but Sasha and I need to hunt, so we can bring you back something. How do you feel about rabbit on a spit?"

"Since I haven't eaten anything since lunch yesterday, anything on a spit would be good. I'll have the fire ready when you get back."

Talon nodded and he and Sasha vanished into the night. Anya helped him gather firewood from a dead tree in the park and when the vampires returned an hour later, they had a roaring campfire lit. Three skinned and gutted rabbits were placed a safe distance from the flames. Conryu was no expert chef, but the smell of roasting meat set his mouth watering.

Dinner was half cooked when Talon said, "I sense something."

Conryu noticed it a moment later, the familiar tingle of Dean Blane's communication spell. "It's okay. I was expecting this call. I asked my teacher to research the Imperials' weapon."

He located the source of the spell and found Dean Blane, Maria, Kelsie, and St. Seraphim looking back at them.

St. Seraphim's white robes practically glowed when she smiled, her blond hair swirling around her pale face. "Did you really locate a Solar Orb?"

"Somebody did," Conryu said. "But I haven't actually seen it yet. Did you find out anything about the elf weapon?"

"I did," St. Seraphim said. "First, it's not a weapon."

Talon hissed. "This thing has resulted in more of my people's deaths than any other force in over a thousand years and you say it isn't a weapon."

Conryu winced. "Guys, this is Lord Talon, my generous host. Lord Talon, two of my teachers, my girlfriend Maria, and Kelsie Kincade."

St. Seraphim cleared her throat. "Please let me clarify. The elves didn't create the Solar Orbs as weapons. They used them to light giant underground farms. The light generated by the orbs is adequate to sustain photosynthesis. At least three known samples were discovered by artifact recovery experts in the last century. How one of them came to your land I can't say."

"There are two more of these devices," Talon said. "Where are they?"

"You'll be relieved to know one is in a museum in Central and the other is believed to be a part of the Iron Emperor's extensive collection," Dean Blane said. "Neither of them present an imminent threat to you or your people."

"That's something I suppose," Talon said. "How do we destroy the one that does present a threat?"

"Destroy it?" St. Seraphim cocked her head. "Elf artifacts are among the most durable items we've ever encountered. An elf-spell glass was dug out from under a fifty-ton heap of rubble and not only did it still function, but there wasn't so much as a scratch on it. I doubt even Conryu's considerable dark magic potential could shatter one of the devices."

The vampire lord tensed. Conryu stepped in. "Prime and I were planning to use a Focused Dispel to negate its magic. Would that be effective?"

"It should work as a temporary measure," St. Seraphim said. "A wizard of sufficient skill should be able to restore its function given time."

"They won't have sufficient time," Talon said. "I'm grateful for your help."

Talon bowed and moved away from the portal. Conryu watched him for a moment then asked, "Any advice for me?"

"Don't get yourself killed," Dean Blane said.

"Seconded," Maria said.

Kelsie nodded, but seemed unable to speak.

"Thanks, guys. I'll be in touch when it's over."

Maria blew him a kiss and the spell ended. He'd be able to give her a real one soon enough, assuming he survived.

When the portal had fully closed Talon said, "How can she say it's not a weapon?"

This wasn't really a debate Conryu wanted to have. "A sledgehammer isn't a weapon, but you can crush someone's head with it easily enough. Let's not get distracted by definitions. How do you want to handle the attack?"

Talon started pacing, clearly still annoyed. "The direct way, I suppose. I'll call my people and we'll advance to the edge of the orb's range and when they fire it up you hit it. If your spell works, we'll attack and if it doesn't we'll run."

Conryu nodded. Not much of a plan, but it would work, hopefully.

9

VAMPIRES VS. DRAGONS

One thing you could say about vampires, they moved right along. Around midnight, three hours after Talon sent out his mental call, fifty of his brothers and sisters had arrived in the park. While Conryu hated to admit it, being surrounded by so many supernatural beings made him a little nervous. Anya and her mother stayed a little ways off to one side. Neither of them would be joining in the fight, Anya because she didn't know much in the way of magic and Sasha because she still hadn't mastered her powers.

Talon explained the situation to his people and invited anyone that wished to leave to do so. Conryu held his expression neutral as he endured the scrutiny of fifty pairs of glowing red eyes. He didn't dare show a moment of weakness. Like Malice Kincade, these were predators of the first order.

In the end no one withdrew. The other vampires were as eager as Talon to avenge their fallen comrades.

"We will draw their attention," Talon said for the benefit of the new arrivals. "As soon as the orb activates, hit it with your spell. After that just stay out of our way."

"Okay, just be sure not to kill the masked wizard. I have some questions I need to ask her."

Talon nodded. "Let's go."

The vampires dematerialized and rushed northeast toward the enemy camp.

Conryu gave Anya a thumbs up and cast, "Father of winds, carry me into your domain. Air Rider."

He streaked into the sky and powered after the others. He turned to Prime as they flew. "A few months ago I was fighting shadow beasts and now I'm teaming up with vampires. Do you suppose the world will ever make some sort of sense?"

"You're looking at it wrong, Master," Prime said. "Both times you were fighting for the party under threat. First the people of Sentinel City and now Talon and his people. From that perspective what you've been doing make perfect sense."

Conryu grinned. "Thanks, Prime. If you sense any of those witches coming at us, let me know."

"Of course, Master, protecting you is my job."

"Mine as well." Kai's voice was barely audible as she spoke through the veil separating earth and Hell. "I shall allow no harm to come to you, Chosen."

Conryu's confidence rose a notch. With those two on his side, how could he fail?

Numerous fires lit the enemy camp. Shadowy figures moved about, tending to whatever needed doing. The center of the camp held a tent big enough to be right at home in a circus. That must be where the czar lived.

Nothing frantic was happening yet, so Talon must not have moved his forces into position. It wouldn't be long though. The vampire had to have sensed Conryu's arrival in the sky above. At least the witches didn't seem to have taken note of him.

As if on cue, a cry went up from the camp and people scrambled around. From the giant tent a silver figure clutching a shining sword emerged. That had to be the czar. He made the dragon-blood warriors Conryu fought look small.

A blinding light burst to life near the camp's western edge. That was his signal.

Conryu flew closer until he spotted a wisp of a woman dressed all in white surrounded by dragon-bloods carrying shields. She held a crystal that glowed like a second sun.

He put his hands a foot apart and chanted, "Darkness dispels everything."

A black sphere crackled to life between his palms. He spoke the spell over and over, pushing his hands closer together with each recitation. After seven times through the spell he could barely contain the power he'd gathered.

With a final, "Darkness dispels everything!" he hurled the now egg-sized blob of darkness at the orb.

The spell struck dead on. Instead of exploding, the dark energy soaked into the crystal, coating it, and cutting off the light until only the fires illuminated the night.

Indistinct figures rushed into the camp.

Screams and machine-gun fire mingled with the crack and flash of lightning. Conryu ignored all of that and searched for the Society wizard. She had to be down there somewhere. Hopefully none of Talon's people would get overzealous and kill her before he questioned her.

"Master, to your right, headed for the southern edge of the camp."

Conryu spotted her a moment later. The masked woman

didn't even try to help the Imperials. Talk about a poor excuse for an ally.

"Talon!" a deep, booming voice bellowed over the chaos. "Face me like a warrior if you dare. Let us settle this, one ruler to another."

"Master! She's opening a portal."

Cursing the distraction, Conryu refocused. A swirling disk of deep blue appeared at the edge of the camp.

Conryu raised his hand. "Break!"

The sphere of dark energy rushed toward the portal and he flew down after it.

* * *

When Roman's challenge rang out over the battlefield, Talon tossed aside the dead soldier in his hands and made his way across the battlefield. He materialized facing the Dragon Czar. Even though they'd been neighbors for centuries, Talon had never seen Roman in person. To say that the dragon-blooded ruler cut an impressive figure would be greatly understating his presence. Roman towered over eight feet in height and he had to be five feet across at the shoulders. Thick silver scales covered his body and his yellow eyes glowed in the dark.

"You think you can beat me in a fair fight?" Talon asked.

Roman laughed. "I don't doubt it for a moment, assuming you have the courage to face me. If by some miracle you win, my army will withdraw and never return. If I win your lands join with mine. Agreed?"

"You only make the offer because your side is losing. In an hour every one of you will be dead anyway."

Talon sensed one of his people approaching Roman from

behind. Before he could give a warning, the czar spun and slashed with his silver sword at the exact moment the vampire took on physical form. The unfortunate woman's head went flying, disintegrating as it went.

Roman bared needle-sharp fangs. "Then again, perhaps you won't all survive. I ask you again, let's settle this like warriors."

Talon nodded. "Tell your people to stop and I'll tell mine."

"Lower your weapons!" Roman bellowed.

Withdraw to the edge of the camp. Talon's telepathic command reached every vampire in an instant. He felt them moving a safe distance away.

He turned his focus back to Roman just in time to lean away from a slash that would have taken his head.

Roman grinned. "You need to be careful."

"Indeed. So much for an honorable battle."

Talon circled right and Roman mirrored him, the silver sword spinning in his hand, ready to lash out in an instant. The tension grew as both warriors waited for an opening.

Talon reversed his direction and in the instant it took Roman to react he lunged. Dark energy crackled around his elongated nails.

He slashed across Roman's midriff, but despite the strength and magic behind them, his claws skated across the silver scales.

Roman's counter-slash breezed over Talon's head, severing the ends of his hair, but doing no real damage.

Talon darted back and his opponent seemed content to let him. He flexed his hands and felt a moment of betrayal. That blow would have gutted a normal opponent. Whatever else Roman was, he wasn't ordinary.

Or aggressive. Given Roman's nature he expected the czar to wade in with a flurry of heavy strikes. Instead he seemed content to hang back and let Talon take the lead. He'd pay for that decision.

Talon dematerialized and swirled around Roman in his mist form.

The czar laughed. "That won't save you."

He drew a deep lungful of air and exhaled. The rush of bitterly cold air sent Talon's immaterial body flying, though the cold didn't bother his undead form in the least.

Talon pulled himself together in time to avoid a quick slash and thrust. He stepped inside Roman's blade and punched him in the throat with every bit of strength his immortal body could muster.

Roman stumbled back a step and pawed at his neck.

Eager to press his momentary advantage, Talon charged in.

The instant he did the sword came swinging in for his head. Only sliding under the blow kept him alive.

As he passed, Talon grasped Roman's knee and squeezed for all he was worth. At last his nails punched through.

Talon ripped back, severing the tendons behind Roman's knee and sending the czar hobbling to one side.

Talon regained his feet and bared his fangs. There was no way Roman could win on one leg.

He took a step toward his limping opponent.

A blinding, burning light burst to life. Talon's body went rigid and he fell to the ground, totally paralyzed.

Roman staggered over, the silver sword gleaming in his hand.

* * *

W hen the orb winked out Lady Wolf knew he'd arrived. No other wizard on the planet had the power to dispel an elf artifact, at least not without an artifact of their own. When the vampires struck she made herself scarce. As soon as she had enough distance between her and the chaos of battle, she opened a portal to the realm of water.

With a hearty good riddance to her captor, Lady Wolf took a step toward the portal. Only to see it collapse before she could enter. Cursing the universe she spun to see the abomination facing her, the Reaper's Cloak covering him from head to toe.

She flicked her wrist at him. "Freeze and rend, Ice Blades!"

Shards of razor-sharp and iron-hard ice formed from the moisture in the air and streaked toward him.

They might have been spit balls for all the effect they had. A handful struck home and were snuffed out in an instant. She'd read the reports describing how Lady Bluejay made out facing him, but hadn't really believed it until now.

Conryu spread his arms. "Do you want to keep going, or can we talk like civilized people?"

"I have nothing to say to you." She was pleased to hear her voice hold steady despite the fear that squeezed her heart.

"That's a shame, because I have a lot of questions. Did you give the czar that orb and if so why?"

"I don't see that it's any of your business."

"Considering how many times the Society has tried to kill me, I'm making it my business. Why don't you just tell me what I want to know? I'm pretty sure my team's going to win and when they're finished, I'll bet I can get one of them to make you talk."

She shuddered at the thought of having one of the undead

in her mind. Far more secrets lurked in there than simply her purpose in the Empire. "Never! Mists rise and conceal, Obscuring Fog!"

Pea-soup-thick mists filled the air, hiding everything. She ran. If she could just get a little distance between them she could portal to safety.

"I can still see you." His voice seemed to come from everywhere in the mists. "Do we really have to play hide and seek? It's kind of embarrassing for a wizard of your strength to be ducking and hiding like this."

She ignored his taunts and kept running, the magic of her spell creating new fog as she went. Maybe he was only bluffing about being able to see her.

The deep, rumbling chant of an earth magic spell filled the air. Lady Wolf took one more step before a stone hand grasped her left ankle.

"No!" She jerked, trying to free her foot.

A second hand grasped her other foot, locking her in place.

He stepped out of the mists, the black cloak swirling around him, hiding his form and making him appear more wraith than man. Conryu gestured and her fog vanished.

Her heart raced and sweat beaded on her lip and forehead.

She was a Hierarch of the Society. No matter what, she would keep her silence. "Do your worst, Abomination."

* * *

Conryu eyed the captive wizard. Did she really think he was going to torture her? Probably, he doubted a Society member would balk at something like that.

Just kill her, the Reaper's voice in his mind urged. *You can drag her screaming soul back and question it to your heart's content.*

"Are you going to pester me every time I use one of your spells?" Having that cold, emotionless voice in his head was getting on Conryu's nerves. Even so it was worth it for the protection Reaper's Cloak offered.

Behind him the battle had fallen silent. Didn't seem like enough time had passed, but he'd never fought with or against vampires, maybe they killed faster than regular people.

If she refused to talk, Conryu could still satisfy his curiosity about one thing. He closed the distance between them and pulled her mask off.

The woman underneath didn't look at all extraordinary. Close to forty, graying hairs mixed in with the dark-brown ones, a few wrinkles around the eyes; she could have been a friend of his mother's. She'd clenched her eyes shut.

He gave the mask a closer look. Ugly thing. "Why do you wear these, Lady... Dog I'm guessing. They look awfully uncomfortable."

She opened her green eyes and glared at him. "It's Lady Wolf. The masks are a sign of power and status in the Society, plus they hide our identities when we're on a mission."

"Oh. Well, your secret's safe, I have no idea who you are."

"I'm not surprised. Most of us go out of our way to be anonymous. Being nice won't get me to talk either."

He shook his head. Of course it wouldn't. "That's fine. I think I'll just hold you prisoner until Talon finishes up then get him to question you."

A flash of light caught the corner of his eye and Lady Wolf smiled. "Maybe you'd better go check on your friends. Seems the Imperials got the Solar Orb up and running."

"Shit!" Conryu leapt into the air and flew full blast toward the camp.

Seconds later he spotted the czar standing over a rigid

Talon. A little ways away one of the witches held the glowing orb.

Kill her. It's the only way.

Conryu refused to accept that. He focused on Talon.

The czar raised his sword and held it poised over the vampire's neck.

"Cloak of Darkness!"

Conryu's spell covered Talon in liquid black.

The blade fell.

The palms of Talon's hands slapped against the sides of the sword, stopping it a foot above his neck.

"No!" Roman roared and bore down with all his strength.

The sword trembled as the two fighters struggled.

A pair of dragon-bloods ran towards the them. That wouldn't do at all.

Conryu landed and slammed his palms to the ground. "Fists of stone, bind and hold, Stone Grasp!"

Hands of rock sprang from the ground at his command and grasped the approaching monsters by the ankles, sending them sprawling flat on their faces.

A pop like a gunshot filled the air when the silver blade finally gave out.

Roman stumbled, his balance lost.

Talon leapt to his feet, the shard of metal still in his hands.

The czar turned just in time to take a foot-long sword through his right eye. He hit the ground, twitched around, and went still.

The light from the orb went out as the witch holding it collapsed. The two dragon-bloods he'd captured went still as well. All around the camp soldiers threw their weapons to the ground and their hands to the sky in hopes of some sort of mercy. If Conryu didn't act quickly he doubted they'd get it.

All around him figures moved in the dark.

Conryu hurried over to Talon, removing the Cloak of Darkness as he went. "Are you okay?"

"Yes, thanks to you." Talon gave the czar's corpse a kick in the ribs. "This bastard wouldn't know an honorable battle if it bit him."

"Well, you won, that's the main thing. The soldiers have surrendered. Could you ask your people not to kill them? I think enough have died because of this monster."

"You would argue for their lives, after all they've done? These men invaded my land and killed my people. Give me one reason I should spare their lives."

"Because you're a better person than the czar could ever hope to be. Besides, sending them back home with a warning should do wonders to dissuade anyone thinking of following in Roman's footsteps."

"You make a strong argument." Conryu noticed the shifting in the shadows had stopped. "You also saved my life and that of my people. For that alone I...we owe you a debt we can never fully repay. I will have them escorted to the pass and sent on their way."

Conryu bowed. "Thank you."

He frowned at the still-unmoving dragon-bloods. No flicker of life filled their chests. A ways behind them the witch was equally unmoving, but her life force appeared strong.

Conryu let his spells fade and walked over to the unconscious witch. He checked her pulse and found it steady. He conjured a light for a better look. Her hair had turned jet black. What could that mean?

"They were connected to the czar when he died," Prime said. "Experiencing the death of another may have been too great a shock for their minds."

"And the dragon-bloods?"

"I'm only guessing, Master, but I suspect they had a closer connection to the czar than the witches and were forced to share his death."

"Would this have happened all over the Empire?"

"Almost certainly."

If that was true then a lot of witches were going to be in serious trouble. They weren't exactly the most popular people in the Empire according to what Anya had told him.

"Oh, shit! I forgot about Lady Dog."

"Wolf," Prime said.

Conryu ignored him and flew at full speed back to where he left the masked wizard. Two puddles of mud and a few footprints marked the spot where he'd left her. He very badly wanted to punch something. Instead he took slow, deep breaths.

Prime flew down for a closer look. "I'd say she used water magic to soften the stone. Not a bad idea since Dispel wouldn't work on it."

"Please don't compliment the enemy. I was sure we'd get something useful out of her. Damn it! We're no better off now than we were."

"You did save the vampires, the soldiers, and ended a war," Prime said. "That's not so bad."

"I meant with the Society. You're right, of course. I'm glad we kept the deaths to a minimum."

"Are we going to return home now?" Prime floated at his shoulder so they were eye to eye.

"No, not just yet. I want to try something."

"I'm not sure this is a good idea, Master."

"Since when has that ever stopped me?"

10

FALLEN EMPIRE

There was nothing more to be found at the site of Lady Wolf's escape so, after taking a moment to recover her mask, he returned to the enemy camp. The vampires kept a close eye on the disarming soldiers. From a few of their expressions it looked like they'd rather be chewing on their necks, but so far everyone had respected Talon's decision.

"Conryu!" Anya ran up and hugged him. She'd made the trip from their hiding place with her mother.

He gave her a pat on the back. "I think we can assume you're safe from the czar."

She glanced over at the body and shuddered. "Is it bad that I'm relieved he's dead?"

"I don't think so, not considering what he put you through. Where's your mom?"

"Off with the others. What are we going to do now?"

"I'm going to have a look at those unconscious witches. I want to see if I can wake them up."

Anya moved away from him and frowned. "Why would you want to wake those horrid women? Better to let them die in their sleep, at least then they won't be able to do any more harm."

"It wasn't their fault."

Conryu crouched down beside the woman that had been operating the crystal. Speaking of which... A quick look around revealed the orb sitting in the dirt about ten feet away. He snatched it up and slipped it into the pocket of his robe. Wouldn't want the wrong person picking that up.

He put a hand over the witch's head. "Reveal."

The glow of light magic surrounded her. No visible injuries. Maybe Prime was right and it really was a backlash from the czar's death.

"Here goes nothing. The gentle light of Heaven washes away all wounds, Touch of the Goddess." He tapped her forehead and the healing energy surged into her.

The woman gasped and sat up. "No. Please. I don't want to. Majesty, I beg yo—"

She fell silent and looked around the dim camp. Her gaze settled on Conryu.

He smiled. "Hi. Don't worry, you're safe now."

She shook her head. "Where am I and how did I get here?" Her English had a worse accent than Anya's, but he could still understand her.

"That's a long story. Why don't you tell me the last thing you remember and I'll try to fill in the gaps?"

"I was in the palace with the czar. He said I was to become a White Witch. I didn't really want to, but he wasn't asking my opinion. He grabbed my face, forced my mouth open, and cut his finger. That's the last thing I remember before you woke me."

"What year was that?" Conryu asked.

"1490 A.E. Why, what year is this?"

"1501. For the last eleven years you've been a White Witch in the service of the czar. When he died it appears everything that happened during that period was wiped away."

She didn't immediately faint, which he took as a good sign. She did sort of gape and stare off into space. Off to one side Conryu spotted Talon watching and given the vampire's enhanced senses probably listening as well.

Conryu went over to him. "You heard?"

He nodded. "Remarkable, if she's telling the truth. Shall we find out?"

Talon moved so smoothly he might have been floating on air. He paused beside Anya and the witch looked up at him. The moment their eyes met her expression went slack. They stayed that way for half a minute before Talon withdrew.

"Well?"

"She's not lying. There's a huge gap in her memories that has been snipped out. I never imagined such an incredible reaction to Roman's death."

"Yeah, me neither. How many White Witches are there in the Empire?"

"I have no idea. Hundreds I'd guess. Why?"

"Right now they're all lying as helpless as she was. We've got to get them out of there."

"We? They're not my people. I owe them nothing. Let the former witches rely on the kindness of their victims."

"You're missing the point." Conryu's frustration grew as he talked. He knew Talon wasn't stupid therefore he was being intentionally difficult. "They were every bit as much victims of the czar as the poor bastards they oppressed. Hell, if things had worked out differently Anya might have been one of the women in need of saving."

They both looked to where Anya was talking quietly with the still-dazed woman. They'd tried to enslave her, but she seemed to hold no grudge against the amnesiac witch.

"You said you owed me a debt you could never repay. Now's your chance to make a down payment. Help me save as many of them as I can."

"What did you have in mind?" Talon didn't dismiss the idea out of hand which was a good start.

"I need to know where I can find the bulk of the witches and I need some of your people to help move them through Hell, preferably tonight, before anyone realizes what's happened."

"I fear when witches and dragon-blood warriors start dropping like marionettes with their strings cut, people will notice. Here's what I'll do. I'll ask for volunteers, but I won't order anyone to help. It's their choice."

"Fair enough, but can I have your assurance that if I bring them here they'll be safe?"

"You have it. We are not given to attacking helpless women."

"No, just to leaving them to die where they lie." Conryu bowed. "Excuse me, I have preparations to make."

He stalked off, leaving Talon staring at his back. Let him stare. Conryu didn't care. He needed help, but the vampire lord didn't seem inclined to provide it. Well, to hell with him. He had resources of his own, hopefully enough to get the job done.

"Was that wise, Master?" Prime asked.

"Probably not. I was thinking of opening a Hell portal here and leaving it open, then making a new one when we arrive wherever the witches are. Maybe I can load them on Cerberus and have Anya take them off."

That wasn't going to work. Anya didn't have the muscle to unload a hundred plus unconscious women by herself and he might need Kai to help him deal with any dangers on his end.

Damn it! He needed at least one more person, preferably two.

"There's another matter to consider, Master," Prime said. "You haven't slept in a day and a half and the only thing you've eaten is a roasted rabbit. And don't get me started on the number of spells you've cast. You're running on fumes."

"I know, believe me I know, but if I don't do this a lot of people will die. I'm almost hoping someone tries to stop us so I can get an energy boost from them."

"Didn't I warn you about that, Master? You've already used Reaper's Grasp once, using it again in such a short period isn't a good idea."

"Conryu?" Sasha appeared a little ways away sparing him from having to continue his argument with Prime. Just as well since it wasn't one he could win.

"Hey, what's up?"

"Talon told us what you're planning. I studied the locations of all the Dragon Temples, that's what they call the barracks where the witches live, during my time with the resistance. I'd be happy to guide you to them."

"Thank you. That would be a huge help. Just out of curiosity, why are you offering to help the witches?"

Sasha let out a long sigh, probably a leftover habit from when she still breathed, and looked back at Anya. "I heard what you said to Talon, about how if things had turned out differently it might have been Anya lying unconscious somewhere, in need of help. It's so easy to think of them as monsters, an enemy that needs to be killed. That's how the resistance always thought of them, but they're also someone's daughter. Every one of those poor women has a mother that misses them. That's reason enough for me."

Conryu grinned, leaned in, and kissed her cheek. "I see where Anya gets her big heart."

Talon formed beside them. "None of the others are willing to help. I guess it's just the three of us."

Conryu cocked his head. "Three? You're volunteering?"

Talon nodded. "Your determination has moved me. What's the plan? We only have five hours before sunrise."

* * *

"Reveal the way through infinite darkness. Open the path. Hell Portal!" The black disk appeared and Conryu led Sasha and Talon through. Lucky for him they didn't require any protection from the dark magic permeating the realm.

Once they were through, he continued to maintain the portal. Focusing his will, Conryu called out, "Dark Lady."

While he waited for his agent to show up, Cerberus came trotting up to the group. All three heads sniffed Talon, who didn't bat a glowing eye, and Sasha, who flinched but didn't complain. Seeming satisfied with what he found, Cerberus ignored them and came over to Conryu.

"Seriously? You snarl at Kai, but not so much as a bark for two vampires?"

Cerberus panted, unconcerned by Conryu's teasing. He rested his head against the demon dog's massive chest and accepted the power that flowed into him. He'd counted on that boost to get him through the night.

Through their link he sensed the Dark Lady approaching. Conryu gave Cerberus a thank you pat and floated around him.

He spotted a point of light in the distance. That was her. It would only take a minute or two for her to reach them.

Talon joined him beside Cerberus. "Friend of yours?"

"My guardian demon. Cerberus has saved my life more than once, haven't you, boy?"

Cerberus gave his happy bark, but kept an eye on the approaching Dark Lady. He'd assumed the two demons had worked out their mistrust, but perhaps not.

"I haven't traveled through Hell in centuries," Talon said. "I can see the borderlands haven't gotten any more interesting."

"Nope, and that's fine with me. Interesting, in my Infernal experience, consists of some demon trying to rend me to bits."

The Dark Lady stopped with a lash of her wings. She looked every bit as beautiful as he remembered with her barely there black dress hugging every curve.

"You look terrible, Master. You haven't been resting enough."

"Thank you," Prime said. "I've been trying to tell him that, but he refuses to listen. Too busy trying to save everyone."

"Enough," Conryu said. "You can both nag me later. Right now we've got work to do. Can you maintain this portal for me?"

The Dark Lady studied it for a moment. "Certainly, you've done all the hard work, I just need to provide a flow of dark magic. How long do you need it open for?"

"However long it takes me to rescue over a hundred unconscious women and ferry them through."

"That's rather vague." She smiled her wicked smile. "Very well, but it'll cost you a kiss."

"If we get through the night in one piece, you can have two."

The Dark Lady swirled her hand around until black flames burst to life. "I have it."

Conryu released the spell and felt better at once. "Okay. Sasha, focus on the nearest temple."

Conryu put a hand on her shoulder and another on Cerberus's flank. A couple seconds later Cerberus gave a bark.

"Got it, boy?"

Another bark. Good.

"Everybody get on. It's time to hunt." Sasha and Talon settled on Cerberus's back behind him and they were off.

It seemed almost no time had passed before Cerberus pulled up. Conryu flew down and opened a viewing portal. On the other side a large white stone building decorated with dragon statues came into view.

He eased closer. No one outside, that was a relief. A set of glass doors led to the interior. He took a step and the view shifted to the inside.

A woman in white lay on the floor, still but breathing. With small movements Conryu scouted the rest of the building. Thankfully no one was up at this time of the night. By the time he finished he'd located nine unconscious witches.

He opened a portal in the lobby and the three of them stepped out. Talon scooped up the unconscious woman and took her back through. It was a risk, sending them back with no protection, but no way could Conryu cast as many Cloak of Darkness spells as he'd need to protect everyone.

While Talon made the first trip, he and Sasha went upstairs. Room by room they collected the witches and ferried them down to the portal. It hadn't taken more than half an hour to clear the building. At this rate they might just finish their mission before morning.

They repeated the process at twelve more temples, rescuing ninety-six witches altogether and meeting no resistance. A throbbing backlash headache built behind Conryu's eyes and it took all his focus to keep from trembling. Even with the energy Cerberus shared with him, he'd nearly reached his limit.

"There's one more place we should check," Sasha said.

Conryu groaned but moved away from Cerberus, "Where?"

"The palace. That place was always crawling with witches."

Probably guards, generals, and lots of other people he didn't want to run into as well, but in for a penny in for a pound.

* * *

To call the Imperial Palace huge would be doing it a grave disservice. It made the Kincade Mansion look like a cottage. It would take forever to search it, especially since someone had placed wards that kept him from opening a portal inside. Instead, he traveled around the perimeter and found a servant's entrance well away from the front door.

Opening what he hoped would be his last portal for a while, Conryu stepped through with Sasha. He tried the door and found it unlocked. No great surprise. Who'd be stupid enough to break into the Imperial Palace?

Beyond the entrance, a long, door-lined hall ran as far as he could see. Everything was painted white with gold accents. He pushed open the first door they reached and soft snoring emerged. He looked inside and found rows of bunk beds barely visible in the dark, servants' quarters most likely.

"Any idea where we should start?" Conryu asked.

"The resistance had a man on the inside, but if he ever sent a floor plan I didn't see it."

"Swell. Prime, can you sense anyone nearby? Maybe we could get some directions."

Sasha choked on a laugh. "Are you planning to just ask?"

"No, I thought you could do it. You're a vampire right? Can't you read their minds?"

"Not yet, I'm new to all this."

He clenched his jaw against the scream of frustration building in the back of his throat.

"Master, there are many humans clustered together at several points throughout the building. It's impossible for me to say which ones are the witches."

"Of course it is. Let's try the middle. That's where the important people usually sleep, right?"

When no one argued, Conryu led the way down the hall past door after door until it widened out into some sort of ball room. A woman in white with brown hair sprawled on the parquet floor. His first witch. Of even more interest to Conryu was a table against the wall with covered trays of cookies on it.

Sasha must have noticed. "I'll carry her back to Talon. You have a snack."

She picked up the unconscious witch and a long slender piece of wood lined with crystals fell out of the folds of her robe. It looked like a testing device. Conryu pocketed it and turned his attention to the food. As Sasha disappeared down the hall with the unconscious witch, he sat beside the tray and picked up a cookie. It wasn't one he'd had before, but it smelled like molasses and at this point he'd have eaten anything not totally covered in mold.

After his third cookie Prime said, "Master, someone's coming."

He didn't even have time to stand up before two men in white uniforms carrying machine guns entered the room.

The barrels went up.

A black sword appeared out of nowhere and sliced the weapons in half. Kai fully emerged from the border of Hell to strike one in the temple with the hilt of her sword and kick the second between the legs. They both collapsed and she silenced the softly moaning man with a second kick to the head. She didn't kill either of them which he appreciated.

Kai sheathed her sword and approached. "Are you well, Chosen?"

"Thanks to you. How did you get in? I couldn't open a portal in the palace."

"I walked in and once inside, the wards didn't seem to prevent me from entering the borderlands."

"Perfect. I've got a job for you. Scout around and find all the witches so we can collect them without searching every corner of this place on foot. We'll wait here for you."

"I would not leave you unguarded."

"Don't worry, I won't be caught off guard again. Hurry now, we don't have long before dawn."

Kai bowed and disappeared.

"Who was that?" He hadn't noticed Sasha's return.

"That was Kai. She's my death-worshipping ninja body-guard. And yes, I know how crazy that sounds, but it sort of encapsulates my life for the past year and change."

Kai emerged from the borderlands a little while later and said, "I've searched the palace and located twenty-three witches, all unconscious. None of them are under guard at the moment, but there are roving patrols. I've taken out three of them between us and the bulk of the witches. Follow me."

They fell in behind Kai and soon enough found themselves in the luxury portion of the palace. Gold-framed art covered the walls and lush white carpet silenced their footsteps. The witches lived in their own area of the palace, each with her own bedroom.

"I'll start ferrying this lot back to Talon," Sasha said.

"There are three more scattered in this area," Kai said.

"We'll handle those and meet you at the portal." Conryu followed Kai out of the living area and down another hall.

Halfway to the end Prime stopped. "Master, I sense powerful magic behind this door."

"We have little time, Chosen."

"A quick look won't hurt anything." Conryu tried the handle and found the door unlocked.

Inside it looked like a museum display. Fifteen pedestals held up small artifacts under glass domes. Each one had a rectangle under it with writing.

"Elf artifacts, Master." Prime floated in. "I've only seen this many in one place once before and that was over a thousand years ago."

"We can't leave them here. God knows what sort of mischief someone might get into with these. Kai, find a bag. I'll gather them up."

She disappeared down the hall without comment. She didn't seem thrilled, but this was too important to leave to chance.

"Reveal." The artifacts glowed in his magic sight, but the glass and pedestals didn't. There should have been defensive wards on something as valuable as these artifacts.

"Do you sense anything, Prime?"

"No, Master. Perhaps with the witches unconscious the magic protecting them has failed."

"Maybe." Conryu opened the first case and took out a ring set with a ruby the size of his pinkie knuckle. Even if it wasn't magic, the gem alone would be worth thousands.

He'd collected eight of the artifacts and was on his way for the ninth when he spotted an empty display. He frowned and tried to read the caption underneath. It must have been written in Russian because he couldn't make heads or tails of it.

"Can you copy this? I want to get Anya to translate."

Prime drifted down even with the placard and after half a minute of staring said, "I have it."

"Chosen." Kai had a little satchel made of a folded cloth. "This is all I could find."

"It'll do."

They gathered up the rest of the artifacts. Kai tried to hand him the satchel, but he shook his head. "You hang on to these for me. If anyone saw me with them, it would lead to questions I don't want to answer right now."

She tied the satchel tight around her waist. "I'll guard them with my life."

* * *

Conryu sat up with a gasp and stared around the clearing. The last thing he remembered was opening one last portal and slumping across Cerberus's back. All around him white-robed bodies lay on the ground as if awaiting burial.

At least his backlash headache was gone. Nothing like a good day's sleep to set a man to rights.

"Back to the land of the living?" Anya walked over and sat

on the ground beside him. "You had everyone a little worried last night."

"Sorry, I've never cast that many spells in such a short period before, not even the day of the attack on Sentinel City." He groaned and spun to face her. "What time is it and more importantly, do you have anything to eat?"

She smiled. "You're in luck, some of Lord Talon's people showed up a few hours ago with plenty of food. If you can wake our guests at least they won't starve. As to the time I'd guess early afternoon, but there are no clocks out here."

Story of his life. Everywhere he went there were no clocks. "How many did we end up with?"

"One hundred and thirty. The one you woke up, Nosorova, seems to be doing well, though she still can't remember anything about her life as a White Witch. It's strange talking to a woman in her thirties who thinks she's eighteen."

He scrambled to his feet and followed her over to a tent someone had set up. Prime floated along beside them, mercifully silent. No doubt the scholomantic would get around to chastising him for his rash behavior later.

"Where is she anyway?"

"Nosorova? Out checking on her unconscious sisters. Why?"

"I found a testing stick at the palace and I was curious to see if she still had wizard potential. Do you think she'd be willing to try it?"

"It couldn't hurt to ask." Anya brushed through the tent flap and he followed along behind.

Inside the tent waited a table lined with coolers. Conryu flipped open the first one he came to and pulled out a bottle of water. The next one held a selection of fruits. He kept going until he reached one packed to the top with sandwiches. He took the first one he laid his hands on, unwrapped it, and dug in. The first sandwich vanished in short order and he started on the second.

When he finally came up for breath Anya asked, "Do you have a plan for our unconscious guests?"

"Assuming I can wake them all up, I figured we'd try to find their families. I imagine they'd be eager to see their daughters again, however long it's been. Once we know their names and where they used to live, it shouldn't be too hard to track them down."

"It might not be that easy." Anya had a bottle of iced tea and took a sip. "The Empire is liable to be in chaos, maybe for a while."

Conryu shrugged and finished his breakfast. "Maybe, but we'll still do our best. Listen to me, assuming you want to help after everything you went through to escape. I'll be happy to take you back to school with me and you can resume your classes."

"I'm not sure I want to go back at all and since no one's after me now I could just as well stay here with Mom. I don't know, I'll talk to her tonight and see what she thinks."

"Cool." Conryu tossed his empty bottle in a handy bin. "I need to head back and talk to Dean Blane and St. Seraphim. Assuming Maria doesn't kill me, I'll be back before dark."

Anya nodded. "I'll be here."

"Master, the translation," Prime said.

"Right." He'd forgotten all about the placard Prime had copied. "Could you tell me what this says?"

Prime flipped open revealing the text he'd copied.

Anya looked it over and said, "Broken elf artifact, function unknown. That's not very helpful, is it? Sorry."

"It's fine, thanks," he said. Inside he cursed his luck. He'd

WRATH OF THE DRAGON CZAR

hoped the information would give him some hint about what the Society intended.

Conryu left the food tent and opened a Hell portal. He felt neither pain nor dizziness. That was a good sign. He doubted it would be necessary to fight, but if he had to he didn't want to faint in the middle of it.

As soon as he entered Hell Prime said, "I thought for a moment last night you really had killed yourself. Why risk so much for complete strangers? Do you have some sort of mental defect?"

"If you call the inability to see someone in trouble and not look the other way a defect, I guess I do. Those women had no choice about what was done to them. They deserve a chance at something resembling a normal life."

"You want to give them what you can't have," Prime said.

"No fair reading my mind."

Cerberus trotted up and barked. A moment later Kai appeared, the satchel of elf artifacts over her shoulder.

Cerberus licked him with a long black tongue.

"I'm glad to see you too. Kai, are you well? We can go back for a sandwich if you're hungry."

"I'm fine, Chosen, thank you. We're trained to go long periods without food. As long as I spend most of my time here, my bodily functions are suppressed."

"I didn't know that. Prime, did you know that?"

"Yes, Master."

"Of course you did." Conryu flew up on Cerberus's back and when Kai had joined him he said, "Take me to the academy."

Cerberus barked and they were off.

Kai put her arms around him and laid her head on his back. "You are a strange one to be Chosen by the Reaper. I've read the histories. The previous Chosen were cruel and indifferent to others' suffering. They used their power to satisfy their hungers without a care for anyone else. Basically the total opposite of you. Do you know why the Reaper marked you?"

"To tempt me, I suspect. He wants me to use his power to kill people, preferably lots of people. He whispers in my ear every time I put on that stupid cloak. If I had another option, I wouldn't even bother with it, but it's too useful a defensive spell to ignore. So instead I do my best not to pay attention to his suggestions. So far it's working pretty well."

"I'm pleased that I was selected to serve a Chosen like you."

Cerberus stopped and let out a bark. They climbed down and Conryu gave him a pat on the flank.

"Do not hesitate to call me if you run into trouble." Kai bowed and backed away.

"Thanks, you're a good friend." Conryu opened a portal and stepped into his room.

* * *

Lady Wolf breathed a sigh of relief when she emerged from the realm of water. The Le Fay Society's primary base of operations was an old Victorian mansion in a remote corner of Wales that had survived the Elf War with minimal damage. As she approached the wrought iron fence, the gate swung open as if welcoming her home.

When Conryu had captured her, she'd feared for a moment that she wouldn't be able to escape, but the fool had left her with nothing more than simple stone bindings holding her in place. It ended up being only a few minutes' work to transmute them into mud and free herself. His inexperience saved her.

She climbed the three steps up to the porch and

approached the whitewashed front door. Like the gate, the doors opened at her approach. The foyer held only a simple table and coat rack. No sound broke the silence. That didn't surprise her. Most of the time the members were out on missions of one sort or another. Lady Wolf was looking forward to a few hours, or if she were fortunate a few days, of peace and quiet.

At the far end of the foyer a long staircase led to the second floor. At the top stood a silent Lady Dragon. Lady Wolf's heart skipped a beat. She hadn't noticed her superior's approach.

Lady Dragon crooked a finger and walked back toward her office. It didn't take a genius to recognize the silent summons. Lady Wolf was a few weeks later than expected so she'd been anticipating a dressing down. She'd also hoped to delay it, but maybe it would be better to have it over with.

She took the stairs two at a time and met Lady Dragon in her office. The plain room wouldn't have looked out of place in any business woman's home. Bookcases and a cherry desk dominated the area. There was no sign of magic present. To a casual visitor the whole house would be at worst considered eccentric, but in no way alarming.

Lady Dragon sat behind the desk. "Where is your mask?"

Lady Wolf blinked. Of all the things she expected her superior to say, that wasn't it. "I lost it to the abomination. I'll create a new one after I've rested."

"No, before we do anything else we'll complete the Ritual of Severing. It would be far too easy for a skilled wizard to follow the psychic link between you and the mask here."

Lady Wolf had forgotten all about the risks of losing her mask. She'd been so eager to escape she hadn't even tried to retrieve it. "My apologies, Mistress."

Lady Dragon waved her hand, dismissing the issue. "The artifact fragment?"

She hastened to get the item out of her pocket. When Lady Wolf put the semi-circle of metal on the desk it hardly looked like anything special.

Lady Dragon ran a finger along its rune-inscribed surface. "At long last. This success makes up for a multitude of sins. Well done, Lady Wolf. Lady Tiger is completing her research as we speak and will join us in the next week or two. All our efforts will soon bear fruit. I can feel it."

A shiver of excitement ran through Lady Wolf. Their long-held dream of seeing Morgana free would at last come true.

* * *

The portal had barely closed behind him when a gust of wind swirled around his neck before solidifying into a tiny girl. The pixie pressed her cheek into his and he smiled. It felt like he'd been gone for more than two nights. Though they had been very eventful nights.

"*Hello.*" It was one of the few words in the language of air he'd learned. "Did you miss me?"

The pixie nodded and hugged his neck.

"Have classes started? I need to talk to Dean Blane."

She nodded again and tugged him toward the door. Conryu allowed the pixie to pull him into the hall and up the steps. They crossed the campus to the main building and went straight to the dean's office. The secretaries only glanced at him before looking away. Was he in that much trouble? Considering everything he'd done, he probably was.

Oh well, he wouldn't change any of his choices. He'd done

what he thought necessary at the time. Conryu knocked and the door opened.

Dean Blane got up from behind her desk, stalked around, and drew a deep breath. He braced himself for the coming tirade.

Instead, he got a hug.

"I'm so glad you're safe," Dean Blane said. "Sit down and tell me everything."

Conryu did as she asked, leaving out only the elf artifacts he'd liberated from the czar's collection. No way was he telling anyone who might pass it on to Malice. The crazy, power-hungry old woman with a dozen artifacts wasn't something he wanted to think about.

"Anyway, I've got a hundred plus unconscious women I need to wake up and doing it one Touch of the Goddess at a time will take too long. I was hoping St. Seraphim might have a different spell I can use. Or maybe she could just come back with me and lend a hand."

"I'm afraid I can't allow that," Dean Blane said. "The teachers are all official government employees and if we got involved in foreign affairs and someone found out it would be like giving official approval. We could end up fired at best and on The Lonely Rock at worst."

"Yeah, I didn't think it would really work, but I wanted to ask. Speaking of the wizard prison, what do you suppose the artifact Lady Dog—"

"Wolf," Prime said.

"Whatever. What do you suppose it does?"

Dean Blane shook her head. "No idea. With elf artifacts the sky's the limit. You can bet whatever they have planned it won't be good for us."

"I almost forgot." Conryu took the crystal-studded wand

out of his inner pocket. "Do you know how to make this thing work? It doesn't seem to react to me."

He tossed it to her and she muttered a spell he didn't recognize. "You need to charge it with light magic to get it started and keep it from reacting to your own magic. Are you planning to use it to test the former witches once you wake them up?"

"Yeah, I wanted to see if they still have wizard potential. Assuming any of them want to pursue that path."

"Why don't you take one of our testers? It'll give you a more accurate reading."

"Cool, thanks. Assuming any of them are interested, can I offer them places at the academy?"

"We only train Alliance citizens. You could ask Malice for special permission, but I don't know what price she'd extract."

"Not to mention she basically told me to stay out of the Empire's business. No, that's not going to work. I didn't free these women from one master only to give them another."

"You really don't like Malice, do you?" Dean Blane asked.

"Do you?" Conryu countered.

She grinned. "No comment. I think St. Seraphim is free first period. Do you want me to call her here?"

"That would be great."

Fifteen minutes later the head of light magic studies breezed into the dean's office. Her white eyes settled on Conryu. "You've been busy I hear."

"Very busy. I've over a hundred unconscious women I need to wake up. Touch of The Goddess works great, but I don't think I can cast it enough times to wake them all before they die of dehydration."

"Touch of The Goddess works on pretty much everything and if there's no physical damage to go with the psychic is complete overkill. How did these unfortunates come to fall unconscious?"

Conryu gave her the short version of what he'd told Dean Blane.

"So, it's backlash from the czar's death. My guess is their minds are stuck in a negative feedback loop. You just need to break them out of it."

"Great," Conryu said. "How?"

"Simple, there's a spell called 'Mass Alert.' It's designed for military applications. Basically it uses light magic to cause a person that hasn't gotten enough sleep to feel fully rested for a short time, say the length of a battle. Anyway, in your situation, it will alter those women's mental patterns, thus breaking them out of the feedback loop. They'll feel a bit hung over for a few hours, but other than that there are no side effects."

"Perfect. Can you teach it to me?"

They spent the next two hours going over and over the spell until Conryu had it down pat.

St. Seraphim left to prepare for her afternoon class, seeming no more perturbed than when she arrived. Nothing seemed to faze her and he found that very reassuring.

"Are you going straight back?" Dean Blane made no effort to try to stop him which he appreciated.

"No, I have one more thing to do. Lunch is about to start, isn't it?"

* * *

The cafeteria was about half full, a little bit bigger audience than he wanted for what he had coming, but that couldn't be helped. He spotted Maria and Kelsie at their usual table. They hadn't seen him so he eased his way over to approach Maria from behind.

Kelsie noticed him, but other than a widening of her eyes gave nothing away.

"Is this seat taken?" he asked.

Maria leapt up and wrapped her arms around him. He sighed and held on until she started to pull away. The moment the hug ended the glare began. "I've been worried sick. What were you thinking, sticking your nose into a war for goodness' sake? You could have gotten killed. Did you even think about that?"

Actually he hadn't thought about it all that much. Probably just as well. "Sorry. On the bright side Anya's mom is safe and the people that wanted her captured are out of power so she's safe as well. All in all a good outcome."

"So where is Anya now, resting in her room?" Maria sat back down and he settled in beside her, throwing a wink at Kelsie who grinned back.

"She's still back there. Now that no one's after her, Anya's not sure if she wants to come back to the academy or stay with her mother. They're going to discuss it tonight."

"So you have to go back?" She sounded more weary than upset.

"For sure. There's still a lot of work to do. I'd offer to bring you along, but until I figure out how to travel through a realm other than Hell, it's too risky." He turned to Kelsie. "Do you want to come, meet some friendly vampires?"

She held up both hands. "I'll pass, thanks."

He grinned. "Okay. If nothing else it looks like you'll get your couch back for winter break."

She brightened. "That'll be nice. Your mom makes the best breakfasts."

"Got that right."

They talked for a while about inconsequential things. Maria had discovered she had a knack for combining water magic and light magic for healing which impressed her teachers. Kelsie was managing with earth magic, but she worried she wouldn't master her spells fast enough to pass the midterm.

For an hour he forgot about vampires, dragon-blood warriors, unconscious witches, and secret societies. Then the pixies came to fetch everyone for their next class and it was time to head back.

11

EPILOGUE

W hen Conryu emerged from the Hell portal back in the vampire's country it was still light out. A group of maybe a dozen people had gathered around the food tent and Anya was talking to them. He walked closer.

"So what we need to do is break down all but the tents we'll need for the refugees. There are a hundred and thirty of them so count beds and mark the tents you're going to keep. When Lord Talon wakes up, he'll have more information for you." She spotted Conryu and waved. "That's all, thanks."

"What was that about?" Conryu asked.

"I don't know. They showed up an hour ago and said Lord Talon summoned them. I wasn't sure what to do, so I put them to work. We need to get this camp cleaned up sooner or later."

"Sooner. St. Seraphim taught me a spell that should wake them all up in one go. Speaking of awake, how's Nosorova settling in?"

"Good, but she doesn't have much stamina yet. She's zonked out in one of the tents."

Conryu cracked his knuckles. "Let's see if we can get her some company."

They walked over to where the unconscious witches – maybe he should think of them as former witches – lay unmoving on the ground.

He took a deep breath to settle himself. The words of the spell were simple enough, it was the intricate motions that really took his focus. When he'd run through the spell in his mind a couple times he cast, "Alarms rattle and rave. Thoughts race like lightning. Mass Alert!"

Like someone had sounded a giant bell, women started sitting up and staring around. Their gazes bounced around, failing to land for more than a second on anything. He caught Anya's eye and nodded left. She went that way and he went right.

One by one they spoke to each woman, explaining what had happened. To a person they all imagined they were eighteen again, even one old enough to be his grandmother. For the newer witches it should be simple enough to wrap their minds around what happened, but how did a sixty-year-old make peace with losing more than half her life?

He didn't know, but Conryu hoped Talon could use his powers to help them. Conryu's part of the job had been easy compared to that.

Gradually, everyone made their way to the food tent. None of them had eaten in over a day so they had to be hungry. By the time the sun had set everyone had eaten their fill and the workers were finished taking down all but the necessary tents. A black mist appeared and Talon and Sasha solidified out of it.

"I see you got everyone up," Talon said.

"Yeah, I had to learn a new spell to do it in one go, but the easy part is done now."

"If that was the easy part, what's the hard part?" Sasha asked.

"Finding everyone's family and getting them reunited. I'm hoping I can work on it Sundays and maybe a few evenings since I really can't skip any more classes."

Talon smiled. "You don't do anything halfway, do you?"

"My father says if you're going to do something, do it with everything you've got."

"A wise philosophy," Talon said. "I'd like to meet your father someday. I suspect we'd get along."

"How about Christmas dinner? You, Sasha, and Anya would all be welcome."

Talon laughed. "A human inviting a vampire to a Christian celebration. That may be a first in my long life. We shall see. And thank you."

"I almost forgot, I brought a magic tester from home." Conryu dug the little device out of his robe and handed it to Talon. "If any of them are interested in resuming a life of magic, they can check themselves out with that."

"I'll let them know."

Anya emerged from the food tent and trotted over. It was time for her to make a decision.

"I'm heading back," Conryu said. "Are you coming or staying?"

Sasha raised an eyebrow. "What's this about staying? You need to learn to use your magic and there's no one to teach you here."

"Now that we're both safe, I don't want to leave you again," Anya said.

"I understand, kiska, but learning to use your magic is

important. When you finish your studies, we can be together again. I have all the time in the world now."

Anya looked away from her mother and chewed her lip, clearly with no idea what she should do.

"I'll be coming back every Sunday to help the former witches find their families," Conryu said. "You could come with me and spend some time with your mother."

Anya brightened. "Would that be okay?"

"Of course," Talon said. "Didn't I tell you before that you'd be welcome anytime? I'm happy to extend that welcome to Conryu as well. He's certainly proven himself a friend to us all."

Conryu bowed. "Thank you, sir."

Anya hugged her mother. "Until Sunday then. I love you, Mom."

"I love you too, kiska. Study hard."

"I will."

Conryu covered her with a Cloak of Darkness and opened a portal. It was going to be a long autumn, but somehow he'd get those women back to their families.

* * *

Lady Wolf was resting and recovering from the Ritual of Severing when the house wards indicated a portal opening nearby. She slipped her replacement mask over her face and left her room. Lady Wolf reached the stairs in time to see Lady Tiger step through the door. She wore crimson robes in the eastern style that hung past her hands and hid every bit of skin from chin to toes. Lady Dragon joined her a moment later.

"What news?" Lady Dragon asked.

Lady Tiger shook her head. "I can't reach the fragment. It's currently being held in the most secure facility in the Kingdom. I doubt all of us together could break through their defenses."

"That is not what I wanted to hear," Lady Dragon said in the tone that usually meant trouble for the person she used it with.

"I know," Lady Tiger said. "But I've worked out a strategy to claim it if we're patient."

"I'm listening." She'd bought herself a momentary reprieve.

"This summer the London Museum of Magic is putting on a display of elf artifacts. The fools imagine they're only displaying the least dangerous ones, as if there was such a thing as a safe piece of elf magic. Anyway, I learned the fragment will be a part of the display. It seems they're hoping to take advantage of the influx of tourists."

"Why?" Lady Wolf asked. "What's happening this summer?"

"It's the Kingdom's turn to host the Four Nations Tournament. Magic fans by the thousands will be pouring into the city. With the proper planning it will be the perfect time to snatch the artifact."

"You've done well, Lady Tiger. And while any delay rankles, we will succeed in the end. I leave this matter in your hands. Complete your mission and I will tell Morgana of your part in her rescue myself. Fail, and I will have you replaced."

"I will not fail. This summer the fragment will be ours."

AUTHOR NOTES

Nothing like a war between vampires and dragon monsters to get the blood pumping. This story was a lot of fun for me to write and I hope you enjoyed it as well. In our next story Conryu gets roped into joining the Academy Team for The Four Nations Tournament. It seems rating aren't what they used to be and he's been chosen as the star attraction. The lethal Lady Tiger is also in London on a quest to obtain the other half of the broken elf artifact. It should be an exciting story and I hope you'll join me. Until next time.

Thanks for reading,

James E. Wisher

ALSO BY JAMES E WISHER

The Aegis of Merlin:

The Impossible Wizard

The Awakening

The Chimera Jar

The Raven's Shadow

Escape From the Dragon Czar

Wrath of the Dragon Czar

Soul Force Saga

Disciples of the Horned One Trilogy:

Darkness Rising

Raging Sea and Trembling Earth

Harvest of Souls

ABOUT THE AUTHOR

James E. Wisher is a writer of science fiction and Fantasy novels. He's been writing since high school and reading everything he could get his hands on for as long as he can remember. This is his sixteenth novel.

To learn more:

www.jamesewisher.com
james@jamesewisher.com